What the press says about Harlequin Romances…

"…clean, wholesome fiction…always with an upbeat, happy ending."
—*San Francisco Chronicle*

"…a work of art."
—*The Globe & Mail*, Toronto

"Nothing quite like it has happened since *Gone With the Wind*…"
—*Los Angeles Times*

"…among the top ten…"
—*International Herald-Tribune*, Paris

"Women have come to trust these clean, easy-to-read love stories about contemporary people, set in exciting foreign places."
—*Best Sellers*, New York

Tuesday's Jillaroo

by

KERRY ALLYNE

Harlequin Books

TORONTO • LONDON • NEW YORK • AMSTERDAM • SYDNEY

Original hardcover edition published in 1977
by Mills & Boon Limited

ISBN 0-373-02184-4

Harlequin edition published July 1978

PRINTED IN U.S.A.

CHAPTER ONE

DAWN was just breaking when Shannon Marshall awoke
the morning after she had boarded the north-western ex-
press in Sydney—a pink, white and gold awakening that
she watched in fascination as the blazing orb of the sun
slowly raised itself over the heavily timbered slopes on the
horizon to disclose a cloudless blue sky above a fairytale
landscape, its searching rays turning the overnight dew into
thousands of glittering jewels. Too excited to go back to
sleep, Shannon pressed her nose to the carriage window
elatedly.

It was all she had imagined it might be. The wire-strung
fences between ironbark uprights; the sheep and cattle
already browsing contentedly amidst the shining grass;
feathery grey-green wattles; pink-tinted, smooth-barked
gums; and occasionally, vast freshly ploughed paddocks
stretching to the distance, the rich chocolate-coloured earth
stark against the surrounding green of grass and tree.

After washing in her compartment's miniature basin she
applied only a very faint covering of make-up to her honey-
gold skin, critically watched by a pair of dark blue eyes
from within their frame of black lashes, which were
matched for colour by the riot of short curly hair covering
her head, and proceeded to pack her belongings into a small
overnight bag. Discovering it was impossible to settle to the
paperback she had purchased at the station bookstall the
evening before, she made for the dining car where she
forced herself to take her time over breakfast, knowing full
well there were a few more hours of travel left before she
reached her destination, and allowed her mind to recall the
unbelievable circumstances which were responsible for her
journey.

It had really all begun one lunch time three weeks ago.

For the second edition in succession the Country Weekly newspaper had carried an advertisement in their Positions Vacant columns. She still knew it by heart. *'Jillaroo/Home Help, aged over 20, required for northern tablelands sheep and cattle property. Must be experienced'*, it had read before giving a postal box number for replies.

Shannon lit a cigarette and leant ruefully back in her seat, gazing through the window unseeingly now as the scenery sped past. That 'must be experienced' had, and still was, causing her many an anxious moment. The trouble was, she wasn't experienced—but she was about to attempt to pass herself off as being so. Not for the first time during the last couple of weeks she sighed and wondered just why she had permitted herself to be placed in such an unwelcome position.

Of course, if Guy Crawford—a good-natured friend from her college days—hadn't chosen the very same coffee lounge for lunch that momentous day, or she hadn't informed him of her intentions, things might have turned out very differently indeed. She would, no doubt, have merely received a politely worded refusal to her application for the post, but as it was, the long arm of coincidence had reached out to enfold her. Not only was Guy's father the manager of the stock and station agency which had placed the advertisement—a fact Shannon hadn't known, since she had never actually met his parents—but the Seymours of Tuesday Creek who had instructed that the position be advertised were apparently family friends of long standing.

At first Shannon had openly doubted Guy's statements, but gradually he had managed to convince her he was telling the truth, and when she had explained that jillarooing was something she had always wanted to do, but had never had the opportunity while her father—her sole remaining parent—had required her almost constant nursing during the last years of his life until his death some three months before—and that she was despairing of ever seeing an advertisement for someone *without* experience—he had gallantly offered to see what he could do on her behalf.

The train thundered across a wooden bridge, but even that change in rhythm couldn't bring Shannon back to the present for more than a second or two before she returned to her gnawing reverie.

How could she have guessed that in his willingness to help her attain the position, Guy would invent some experience for her? When they had agreed to meet at the same place the following day in order that he might let her know what had occurred when he had spoken to his father, she had only been interestedly anxious about the outcome, but when Guy arrived with his father in person at their arranged meeting, winked at her conspiratorially and said in a forestalling rush, 'We thought it a good idea if Dad came with me to see you as he's off to South Australia tomorrow and won't be back until late next week. I've already told him about your twelve months on Atyimba in Queensland, so there's no worry about your not being experienced enough,' she had felt herself going wide-eyed in something akin to horror as his meaning had penetrated her unsuspecting mind.

The memory still had the ability to send cold shivers down her spine. But what could she have done about it? Tell the truth and brand Guy an outright liar in front of his own father? She couldn't have repaid his efforts in such a callous way! And when, after he had managed very subtly —and very cleverly, Shannon had to admit—to either answer any of Harold Crawford's questions for her, or to prompt her in the right direction, she found she was actually being offered the post, she didn't know whether to be ecstatic or dismayed.

On the one hand it had been exactly what she wanted— but on the other, well, to say the least, she hadn't been happy with Guy's or her own subterfuge. However, Mr Crawford had been waiting for an answer to his query as to when she would be able to start and, impulsively, she had done a rapid mental calculation, irreversibly burnt her bridges behind her, and suggested today.

A wry smile tugged at the corners of her mouth as she tried to remember all the information Guy had attempted to cram into her brain so that her total ignorance wouldn't be too apparent, and the rushed shopping spree for hard-wearing denims, comfortable check shirts and elastic-sided boots, the purchase of which had depleted her bank balance to the extent that after she had bought her ticket for the train she now had only a couple of dollars left between her and destitution.

Abruptly she hunched her shoulders and pushed the disquieting thoughts away. There was no turning back now and she should be looking for reasons to be pleased with the result rather than the reverse. She could, of course, have refused the post when Mr Crawford had offered it to her, but that would only have made them all look rather foolish after Guy had taken such pains to impress upon his father how keen she was to go—which certainly wasn't an invention—and in true Australian fashion she had decided to take the gamble. As she had told Guy, it was something she had always wanted to do, and if a willingness to work and learn had anything to do with it, then she would do her utmost to see that Mark Seymour, her new employer, had no cause for complaint.

By the time Narrawa finally came into view—the closest station to Tuesday Creek—Shannon was hovering in the corridor suspensefully, eager to set foot on the long platform with its newly painted buildings and tubs of bright zinnias and mignonettes. She was only one of a dozen or more passengers who alighted from the train and began making their way into the station office to await delivery of their cases from the luggage van. Shannon handed in her ticket and stood gazing about her uncertainly, not knowing who to look for as Harold Crawford's secretary had only informed her that she would be met by someone from the property, and seeing the rest of her travelling companions gradually leaving the station, either alone or in company. An affable porter brought her two cases from the van and deposited them next to her, bidding the time of day cheerily before returning once more to the train for another load of goods.

Another few minutes had passed before a dusty and obviously well-used utility swung into the station yard in a flurry of scattered pebbles and came to a halt almost directly in front of her. A tall young man in his middle twenties, brown-haired and brown-eyed, dressed in faded jeans and a blue and white checked shirt, emerged and strode towards her, an engaging smile spreading over his face.

'Shannon Marshall?' he queried with a slight frown of doubt replacing his previous smile, but upon her affirmative nod, 'I'm Pete Seymour, from Tuesday Creek—Mark's stepbrother. Sorry to be late, but I was—er—waylaid in town while sending off the mail.'

By the ready grin that came into play at his 'waylaid' it wasn't hard for Shannon to guess that it had been a female who had detained him and give him back a sparkling smile of understanding which had him watching her consideringly before shaking his head in disbelief.

'I'll give a month's wages to be there when Mark sets eyes on you,' he told her cheerfully.

'Why's that?' Shannon couldn't keep the surprise from her voice.

His head tilted contemplatively as he studied her in detail. 'Well, you sure don't look like any jillaroo I've ever seen before,' he drawled wryly. 'And I'll take a bet that Mark hasn't either!'

Shannon looked down at herself in something close to dismay. Why, she'd thought her denim flared slacks, together with matching battlejacket and printed T-shirt, just the thing to arrive in. Not too cityfied, nicely middle of the road, you might say. Her platform sandals could perhaps, if one felt that way, be described as a little far out, but surely they hadn't expected her to arrive in bib-and-brace overalls with a stockwhip thrown over one shoulder?

Again she questioned, 'Why?' followed by, 'What's wrong with the way I look?'

'There's certainly nothing wrong with your looks,' he replied instantly with an admiring grin. 'That's just what I'm getting at—our jillaroos aren't usually as attractive as you are.'

'Oh!' Shannon flushed at the unexpected compliment, but his words were causing her no little anxiety. It had never occurred to her before that her looks might give rise to the very suspicions she most wanted to avoid regarding her ability to undertake the work she had chosen to do, and she stared at him with a slightly despondent air.

Upon seeing the worried look on her face Pete began to laugh. 'Never mind, Shannon, I'm positive no one on the property will be complaining—least of all Mark!' he assured her with an encouraging grin. 'I've never known him to be averse to having a pretty face around before.'

This comforted her a little, although not too much when she considered all the circumstances surrounding her deception, but she made herself smile back at him as naturally as she could before he began swinging her luggage into the back of the ute.

'Right, let's go,' he said, switching on the ignition after seeing Shannon safely inside the vehicle and easing himself into the driver's seat. 'We should make Tuesday in time for lunch, if you don't object to a bit of fast driving.'

'I don't mind,' Shannon agreed equably, noting the easy assurance with which he handled the ute, and prepared to accept that he knew what he was doing, then, with her face turned quizzically towards him, 'Tuesday, you said? Is that just a shortened version of Tuesday Creek?'

Pete shook his head. 'Uh-uh, Tuesday Creek's the township. Tuesday Park is the name of the station, but for convenience we usually abbreviate it to Tuesday only.' He flicked her a quick grin. 'No prize for guessing how either of them came by their names! It was, of course, a Tuesday when they stumbled across the creek—and the property was christened likewise—it being the same Tuesday when our great-grandfather first started marking out the boundaries. In those days the land where the town now stands used to belong to the Seymours too, but around the turn of the century old Grandad, who never liked to see an opportunity slip through his fingers, realised the need for some sort of centre to serve the district, and divided that portion of the property into saleable lots. Made a fortune from it within a few months, the cunning old fox,' he laughingly decried his forebear.

'And the property's still in the same family,' Shannon mused aloud. 'Have all the Seymours been graziers?'

'Every last one of them,' he confirmed blithely. 'Although there have been some pretty hard times down through the years, I don't think anyone has ever thought of selling out. Must be in the blood, I reckon.'

Shannon nodded her head and looked about her interestedly. They had passed through the centre of town while Pete had been talking and she noted that it was quite a lot larger than she had expected, but now they were leaving the outskirts behind and the old ute was picking up speed as they drove out along the bitumen highway. For a few minutes neither of them spoke, content to watch the scenery slipping by, but then Shannon turned again to her companion.

'How many people actually live on the station?' she asked.

Pete's eyebrows rose as he attempted a quick summing up. 'Thirteen adults—that's including you—and the four children, at the moment. It varies from time to time, of course. Sometimes there's more, sometimes less.'

'Good heavens! Am I supposed to do the cooking for *all* of them?' she enquired, round-eyed. In her anxiety to obtain the post she had never given a thought to the number she might be expected to cater for. That was some jump from cooking for her father and herself to feeding seventeen.

'No, no!' Pete thankfully put her straight right away. 'Betty Lovett, the wife of one of our stockmen, does the cooking for the men. You'll only be doing it for the homestead. That's ... let's see ... Mark; my mother; my sister Christine, and her two kiddies, Davey and Jane; yourself and yours truly. Normally the two jackaroos would also be eating at the homestead, but with Chris and myself at home they've gone back to eating in the men's quarters.'

'You and your sister don't usually live on the property, then?'

'Not usually,' he endorsed. 'Chris and her husband, Paul, have a station up in the gulf country in Queensland, but young Davey broke his arm falling out of a tree and they couldn't get it to heal, so the doctor recommended she bring him south. He's as right as rain now, so I expect they'll be going home soon. Chris says she couldn't stand our cold winters anyway after having been gone for so long. As for myself, after completing four years' jackarooing and two years at agricultural college, I'm having what you might call a working holiday at home for a few months before taking up the position of working manager on a station further west.'

The miles were rushing by now. 'And just who does Betty Lovett cook for?' Shannon asked.

'Her two kids, and the normal station staff.'

'Which consists of ...?' she queried innocently.

His forehead furrowed into a frowning look of incomprehension. 'Surely you would know that, having worked as a jillaroo before,' he threw the onus back on to her for an explanation.

Oh, God, she had nearly given herself away on that one! She was going to have to be a lot more careful if she wasn't to make any more mistakes before she had even arrived at the property. Shannon gulped hastily and gave a tolerably light laugh.

'Of course,' she agreed as nonchalantly as she could. 'What I should have said was—which consists of ... whom? I was—um—really meaning their names,' she managed to evade the question.

'Oh, I see,' Pete smiled back at her. 'You really had me going there for a moment. You sounded as if you'd never been out west before.' Which did absolutely nothing to boost Shannon's failing confidence. 'Well, there's Jim Colewell and Wade Reardon, the stud and stock overseers respectively; Gordon Lovett and Rex Tatnell, the stockmen; Trevor Dobson's the station hand; while Tony Gates and Don Ferguson are our two jackaroos.'

Inadvertently Pete had just told her exactly what she had wanted to know, but something else he had also disclosed made her very thoughtful. He had classified the stockmen, station hand and the jackaroos into three distinct categories, and as she had always believed that they were just different terms to describe the same person it made her realise all too clearly just how ignorant she was on these matters, and the idea of bluffing her way through with regard to her experience was beginning to seem extremely ludicrous—no matter what Guy had said to the contrary—and her buoyant spirits of earlier that morning began sinking unrelentingly to zero.

'You've suddenly gone very quiet. Anything wrong?' Pete broke into her reverie with a swiftly enquiring regard.

'No, no,' Shannon quickly disclaimed her fears. 'I—I just wondered if one of the names rang a bell, that's all,' she fabricated on the spur of the moment. 'But on second thoughts, it was a—a Don Fegan I knew,' she laughed huskily, and hoping for a change to a safer subject, went on slightly breathlessly, 'From what you said earlier, I gather your stepbrother's not married,' with a questioning look.

'Not yet,' Pete returned noncommittally.

'And your mother? Doesn't she do any of the cooking at the homestead?'

'Who? My mother?' he counter-questioned with such incredulity that Shannon panicked into thinking she had again unwittingly put her foot in it, and heaved a sigh of relief when he added, 'No, she's an artist, and housekeeping is something that's just not included in her realm of consideration. She's away in a world of her own most of the time—out with her paints and easel—considering colours and lines. I sometimes wonder if she even realises the rest of us are around,' he grinned indulgently.

Shannon had to smile at his description, but a second later a recollection struck her. 'Your mother's not *Nola* Seymour, is she?' she quizzed doubtfully.

'You know her work, then?'

'Do I? Who doesn't?' They were unequivocal statements rather than questions. 'I can still remember, years ago, when my father took me to a showing of her paintings at one of the galleries in Sydney. I sometimes think it was the vivid feeling of action that she gets into her scenes that first gave me the idea of becoming a jillaroo,' she confessed self-consciously. 'I've never forgotten one she'd painted of a man and a young boy squatting on their haunches around a campfire, the man with his hands clasped round a mug and the boy with his fingers held out to the flames, while the mist swirled about them and the rising sun turned the hides of the cattle in the background a deep dark red. I always had the impression that if I stood there long enough the figures would start to move, it was so lifelike.'

'Umm, I know what you mean. That was Dad, and Mark

when he was a kid. It still holds pride of place in Mum's studio—one of the few canvases she won't sell. She's always sketching the stockmen and the jackaroos when they're working, so don't be surprised if you suddenly turn round one day and find her sitting behind you, pad and charcoal in hand, faithfully recreating your every action for posterity,' he smiled.

'Goodness, you mean I might become one of those "Subject Unknown" paintings that you see sometimes?' Shannon chuckled infectiously.

'More than likely, because Mum usually forgets a name as soon as she's heard it,' he laughed with her. 'Everyone is "dear" to my mother. That way she doesn't have to put herself to the trouble of recalling individual names and it works equally well for both sexes.'

'She sounds delightfully vague.'

'She's certainly that all right,' conceded Pete with an emphatic nod of his head.

More miles were clocked on the gauge and then they rounded a bend in the road and a small cluster of buildings lay before them—nowhere near the size of Narrawa and not nearly as busy—but as they sped down the single street Pete was called upon to return numerous called greetings and casual salutes.

'Tuesday Creek,' he informed Shannon laconically. 'It's okay for the necessities, but don't count on them having anything out of the ordinary. You usually have to make a trip into Narrawa for that.'

Shannon nodded her head in acceptance and began to look about her with renewed interest, surmising that it wouldn't be long now before they arrived at the property. As it was, only another quarter of an hour had passed before Pete slowed the ute and turned through a curving brick entranceway, one side of which was adorned with a beautifully ornate sign advertising *Tuesday Park Poll Here-*

ford Stud and decorated by a painting of a most natural-looking reddish brown and white Hereford bull being led by a rope through the ring in his nose.

Beside the gravelled road pencil pines pointed skywards while the timber stained fences and orderly paddocks gave the place an atmosphere of more-than-comfortable prosperity. Then, as they followed the last curve in the track, the homestead and outbuildings became visible, situated on the top of a slight rise immediately in front of them.

The house itself was a long, low white building, completely symmetrical on either side of the steps that led on to a wide verandah where, apart from the imposing main entrance, french doors permitted access to the internal rooms, and which was surrounded by a delightfully simple fretwork of wrought iron which matched the delicate creeper-covered supports for the low-slung red hip roof. There were at least two other cottages that could be seen to the left of the main homestead, and the outbuildings seemed too profuse for Shannon to even guess at most of their functions.

Pete brought the ute to a halt in front of the wide steps and swinging her legs out as he opened the door for her, Shannon rose to her feet and nervously rubbed the palms of her hands down the sides of her slacks. Now that she had finally arrived things didn't seem quite so easy as they had in Sydney and she wondered whether she was expected to meet her employer immediately, or if she would be allowed a little time to settle in before the meeting took place.

Apparently it was to be the latter, causing Shannon to expel her subconsciously held breath in relief, as a young woman in her late twenties crossed the verandah and lightly skipped down the steps towards her, saying, 'I'm sorry Mark isn't here to welcome you himself, but he should be back later this afternoon. I'm Christine Woodman—Mark and Pete's sister.' Then, 'My husband's always saying he thinks he'll put on a jillaroo—looking at you, I can see the reason why,' she chuckled, holding out a hand which Shannon took in a friendly clasp.

Pete ambled past with two cases, heading for the doorway. 'Shannon Marshall, meet my sister, Chris,' he completed the introduction for them with a grin. 'But watch yourself, Shannon, or she'll talk your ear off.'

Chris spread her hands wide expressively. 'Who could blame me if I did after having to put up with your company for so long?' she grimaced in sisterly fashion at his retreating figure. 'Anyway, come on in,' she ushered Shannon towards the steps leading on to the verandah. 'I expect you'd like a wash and tidy before lunch. I got it ready a little earlier today as Mark won't be back and, if you're anything like me, you probably had an earlier than normal breakfast on the train and now you're feeling distinctly peckish.'

Having admitted to the truth of this Shannon followed Chris into the homestead—dark and cool after the sunlight outside—and down the hallway to a very prettily decorated bedroom where her cases had been neatly stacked at the end of the bed.

The furniture was of a light, shining Queensland maple and combined with the pale cream walls and apple green drapes to give the room a bright, open effect. Besides the bed with its fluffy cinnamon-coloured chenille bedspread and the usual bedroom furniture, there was also a writing table and chair set by the doors which led on to the side verandah, as well as a small cretonne-covered sofa next to some bookshelves along one wall. It was a very pleasant room and Shannon couldn't help comparing it to the rather depressing bed-sitter she had left behind in Sydney with a very favourable reaction.

'The bathroom's two doors down on the right,' Chris was saying, 'so I'll leave you to settle in while I go and check that everything's right for lunch. Okay?'

Shannon nodded happily but called out as the older girl

turned through the doorway, 'Where will I find the kitchen when I'm finished?'

'Last room on the left at the bottom of the hall. You won't be able to miss it because I clatter a lot,' was supplied with a catching grin.

CHAPTER TWO

ONCE Chris had left, Shannon swiftly unlocked her cases and began placing her small wardrobe of clothes in the appropriate receptacles, congratulating herself on the fact that the first family she had chosen to work for in the country were proving to be so agreeable. Mentally she crossed her fingers and hoped that could still be said after she had met her employer.

A quick wash in the aqua and white tiled bathroom and a disciplinary combing of her curly hair completed her toilet before she made her way to the kitchen where Chris was putting bowls of various salad vegetables on to the divider prior to taking them into the dining room.

Obviously it hadn't been long since the kitchen had been entirely renovated, as the equipment and facilities were up to date beyond anything that Shannon had expected to find, and with the light playing on to the very pale orange and lemon cupboards, bringing vivid life to the copper ornaments arranged so artistically round the walls, as well as to the orangey-brown clinker bricks that supported the divider between the two rooms, it was an area where Shannon knew she would enjoy creating more of the dishes her father had so relished.

Between the two of them it didn't take long to have the

table laid and Pete had only just entered the room when he was followed by a well-built woman in her late fifties, her fading light brown hair cut remarkably short into deep waves, and her blue and white striped dress bearing some definite paint smudges around the hem.

'Oh, dear,' she murmured softly on catching sight of Shannon. 'Why didn't you tell me we were having visitors, Chris? I removed my smock, but I would have changed my dress too if I'd known.'

'Not visitors, Mum,' her daughter shook her head in mock exasperation. 'This is Shannon Marshall—our new jillaroo. Don't you remember? Mark told us she would be arriving today.'

Mrs Seymour turned light blue eyes on the new employee and gave a particularly sweet smile. 'I think I can recall him saying something to that effect now,' she said as they all took their seats at the table. 'I'm very pleased to meet you, my dear. I hope you'll be very happy here.'

'I'm sure I shall, thank you, Mrs Seymour.' Shannon's reply was confident. She only hoped it wasn't going to be proven later to have been overly so!

For a few minutes there was silence in the room as brimming plates and dishes were passed and received across the table until everyone had what they required and, in the act of putting her fork to her mouth, Mrs Seymour suddenly remarked to no one in particular, 'I expect Mark will be pleased.'

Her son and daughter exchanged covert grins, clearly used to this obscure type of opening gambit, but it was left to Chris to query, 'Why's that?' with a reasonably straight face.

'Well...' For a time it seemed her mother had completely forgotten what she had been about to say, but then her voice firmed and she continued, 'Because the last jillaroo we had here, and she was only a tiny thing too, was so terribly clumsy. She would keep breaking things all the ·

time. If she was like that at home her parents must have been very relieved when she left,' she mused vaguely before turning to Shannon. 'You look much more capable, my dear, and I'm sure Mark will appreciate not having to keep such a close watch on *you* all the time,' she finally got around to explaining why she thought her stepson would be pleased.

'Mmm, that's why Mark was so insistent that Harry send us someone who's already had some experience,' Pete added his own information on the matter. 'Although I wasn't here at the time, I understand that the last of your predecessors, Shannon, managed to put Mark off first year jillaroos for life. Not only was it a daily event for her to drop or break something in the homestead, but the second time she was let loose on the tractor she promptly proceeded to plough it into the stockyards, and, to cap it all off, when they finally got her to back it out again, she immediately reversed it into Mark's new car! So, as you can imagine, Mark will be pleased, and relieved I might add, to know that you have all your first year mistakes behind you,' he grinned encouragingly.

But not encouragingly enough, for all Shannon could do in response was to swallow and smile weakly while her spirits sank to their lowest ebb yet—after those few choice disclosures they had easily managed to descend below zero —as she realised, yet once again, the almost formidable task she had set herself in attempting to pass for an experienced worker. What did she know of tractors? Come to think of it, what did she know about *any* farm machinery whatsoever? She couldn't even drive a car, let alone operate a tractor, and deep inside her she could feel a sneaking sympathy for her predecessor who had made such chaos out of her attempts to do so.

The rest of the meal passed safely enough, however, and apart from Mrs Seymour's, 'You don't happen to paint, do you, dear?' to which Shannon could only give a negative reply, causing the older woman to appear to lose interest in the rest of the conversation, there were no other instances which gave Shannon reason to regret her impulsive action in accepting the position.

After lunch, while the two girls were stacking the used plates in the dishwasher, they heard hoofbeats in the yard, but on peering through the window Shannon gave a sigh of relief when she saw that it was only Pete riding down towards the stockyards, and promptly gave herself a good mental shake. It was ridiculous letting the forthcoming meeting with her employer worry her so much. After all, she had the letter of introduction which Mr Crawford had written for her and it probably wouldn't even occur to Mark Seymour to question her as regards her supposed experience.

During the afternoon Chris took her on a tour of some of the outbuildings; the stores shed where there were so many different sacks, bags, drums and plastic containers that Shannon couldn't even hazard a guess as to what they were all used for; the machinery shed with its complicated and overawing equipment all neatly arranged; the shearing shed, silent now, but which later in the year would ring with the sound of protesting sheep, booted feet on the wooden floors, the continuous noise of the shears, the creaking of the presses, and by no means least, the sound of men's shouting and, as often as not, cursing voices.

Next came the sheepyards with their loading ramps and a maze of pens, races, and gates which opened and closed in all manner of directions. Here she met Trevor Dobson, the station hand. Only a few years her senior, dressed in faded and dirt-stained jeans with an equally faded fawn shirt, a slightly worse-for-wear hat jammed squarely on his head and dusty stockboots on his feet, he was busily replacing one of the cross bars in the yards.

Then it was on to the stables and tack room, and although most of the stalls were empty at that time of day,

Shannon enjoyed the minutes they spent with each remaining horse as they whinneyed their appreciation of the attention the girls gave them.

On the way down to Betty and Gordon Lovett's cottage they passed the single men's quarters, as well as the bails where the station's dairy cows were brought in night and morning to provide milk for the seventeen residents on the property and to feed any calves which might have been orphaned.

Betty was a woman of about the same age as Chris and who also had two children, but hers were both boys and younger than Chris's two, who were old enough to attend school. At the moment they were playing with a ball in the yard, so the three women were able to enjoy a short afternoon tea and some companionable chatting before it was time for Betty to begin preparations for the men's evening meal.

Glancing at her wrist watch on their way back to the homestead, Chris uttered a gasped, 'Good grief, look at the time! If I'm not careful I'll be late picking my own two up from school.' And as she began hurrying across to the garage, 'Would you like to come for a drive with me, Shannon? Or would you prefer to stay here?'

'No, I'll come with you. Is it very far?' as she kept pace and slid into the passenger seat of the iridescent dark green station wagon.

'Only about five miles,' Chris told her, backing the vehicle out and swinging it around to face down the slope before changing gear and moving along the roadway. 'It's a one-teacher school—there are only sixteen pupils in all, ranging from kindergarten to sixth class—but my two kiddies thoroughly enjoy it. At home, of course, they have correspondence lessons and it's just not the same as having a whole class of other children about you. I think they're going to find the change just a little bit disagreeable when we return,' she smiled, and slowed to turn out through the gateway and on to the main road where they picked up speed again.

Immediately they pulled up in front of the little white-painted weatherboard schoolhouse set beneath great spreading oak trees, a vast expanse of green grass for a playground and surrounded by a white picket fence, Shannon could understand why Chris's children might be reluctant to leave when the time came. It was a far cry from her remembered image of the bitumen-paved playground and coldly clinical brick and glass school building that she had attended as a child in the city.

Soon all the children came tumbling out of the building together, shuffling and kicking their feet through the autumn fall of leaves from the oaks, and calling to their friends on the way to the gate. Davey, a brown-haired, blue-eyed copy of his mother, reached the car first and after tugging open the rear door had hardly managed to scramble inside before his proud, 'I made two home runs in softball today, Mum!' was made public. In a matter of seconds a demure little blonde with extraordinarily large brown eyes pushed in after him and announced in the same tones, 'I got a home run today, Mummy!'

Chris turned with a smile to her young offspring to offer her congratulations, adding, 'But before you tell me any more, I think you'd better say hello to Shannon. She's come to work on Uncle Mark's property.'

This duty shyly complied with, the rest of the journey was taken up with excited recountings of the various happenings that had occurred during their school day and no sooner had the car been put away and the homestead reached than they had consumed a glass of milk and some buttered biscuits each and were dashing across the yard to play with Luke and Adrian Lovett.

The light was just beginning to fade from the evening sky and Chris's lemon chicken—which she had adamantly refused to allow Shannon help prepare, saying, 'There's plenty of time for that yet. Settle in first,'—was starting to give off an unbelievably appetising aroma by the time the first clatter of horses' hooves and the sound of men's voices could be heard in the yard. Shannon moved closer to the windows and tried to peer surreptitiously between the curtains, hoping a glimpse of her employer might perhaps provide her with a clue as to his disposition, but it was too dark to make out anything more than indefinable shapes and when Chris turned on the kitchen light it was impossible to see anything outside at all.

It wasn't long, however, before the voices became clearer, followed by the sound of heavy feet crossing the verandah, and Pete, his denims spattered with mud from hip to ankle, swung into the kitchen with another man close behind him—his drills having fared no better from the mud than Pete's clothing.

'Spent the last hour dragging one of the steers out of the creek. Lovely way to finish the day,' Pete explained their condition with a grin, but Shannon only heard him with one ear, her whole attention focused on the man beside him and confirming her worst fears.

This was the *boss*! There was no doubt in her mind about that! It was stamped all over him; the authority, the self-assurance, the sheer force of personality, and the nerves in Shannon's stomach curled apprehensively at the thought of her trying to deceive this man.

In his early to middle thirties and standing well over six feet, with an extremely broad and muscular build to match, he was quite easily the most overpowering example of the dominant male Shannon had ever met. The face returning her gaze so intently was ruggedly good-looking rather than handsome—the square, resolute chin and straight nose depicting sheer strength more accurately than mere male beauty. The eyes were an unusual shade of tawny-hazel beneath slightly crooked brows, while the whole teak brown visage was topped by loosely waving black hair. However, it was the firm shapely mouth with its fascinating look of competence that caught and held her attention the longest.

In turn, she was subjected to the most sharp-eyed scrutiny she had ever had to suffer and found herself flushing rosily under the so very thorough regard until Chris broke in brightly to perform the introductions and quipped afterwards with a teasing face, '*He's* the boss!'

Oh, I'd already worked that one out for myself, mused Shannon ruefully, as her slim fingers were grasped by a strong, hard hand that sent nervous shivers down her spine and from which she broke contact as soon as possible without openly appearing rude.

His, 'Glad to have you with us, Shannon,' was spoken in a deeply pleasant voice, but the tone was so perfunctory that her answering, 'Thank you, Mr Seymour,' came out with a betraying huskiness that, to her own ears at least, gave the following, 'I'm glad to be here,' very little semblance of credibility.

'You have a letter of introduction from Harry Crawford, I believe?'

The question took her somewhat by surprise—she hadn't really expected him to ask for her reference quite so soon—but now that he had she found herself replying eagerly, 'Yes, that's right,' and hurrying along the hallway to her bedroom to retrieve it before anything further could be said.

When she returned with the envelope a few minutes later the two men were already near the doorway and with an almost imperceptible nod of acceptance and a cool-sounding, 'Thank you,' Mark Seymour took the letter from her outstretched hand and continued down the hall with a long determined stride.

Shannon watched his departing figure thoughtfully. Perhaps, once he had read the letter, she would be able to feel more secure in her position. Was Mark Seymour usually this short with all new employees? She hunched her shoulders lightly. Maybe it was only as Pete had suggested at the station—that at first glance her looks had given him cause for surprise. Or perhaps it was only her imagination and his brusqueness had been brought about only by their last time-consuming job of the day.

Both men had showered and changed by the time the family sat down to dinner and for the first five minutes Shannon thoroughly enjoyed her meal. Then Mark began his seemingly innocent questioning.

'Do you paint, Shannon?' was the first one which brought a frown to the surface as she turned to look at him in puzzlement for his choice of query, but it was Mrs Seymour who answered for her.

'No, she doesn't, dear. I asked her that myself at lunch-time,' she said amiably, and her light blue eyes roved over their newest employee consideringly. 'She would make a very good subject though, don't you think?'

Shannon could feel the heat rising in her cheeks at this matter-of-factly spoken comment which Pete's, 'I'll say!' in laughing agreement did nothing to dissipate. But she noticed that Mark offered no acknowledgment of the remark other than the slight lifting of what seemed to her one rather doubting eyebrow.

'I see you worked on Atyimba for some time. Did you like the work?' came next, blandly.

Now they were getting closer to home and Shannon drew a deep steadying breath before replying with a valiant smile, 'Yes, very much so.'

'And you would have met George Yuille while you were there, of course?'

Her smile faded abruptly. Would she? Why? Dear God, don't tell me he works here, she pleaded silently, beseechingly. Coincidences couldn't be that great, could they?

'The manager on Ten Wells station, next door,' Pete unwittingly supplied her with a little more information. 'Surely you must have met him.'

'Oh ... yes...' she began as if his presence was slowly being recalled to mind.

'The tall feller with ash-blond hair.' Another clue was obligingly added.

'The one who's always sunburnt?' Shannon prompted quizzically. That would be a fair guess, wouldn't it? because the Queensland sun wouldn't be gentle on the pale skin which normally accompanied such hair colouring.

'Now you've got him!' Pete congratulated her with a grin. 'What's he doing these days?'

Shannon's mind raced chaotically. What would he be likely to be doing? She decided on a safe return and made the comment, 'Much the same as usual,' in a wry tone.

'Still telling those corny jokes, eh?' Pete laughed.

'As always,' she smiled with him in relief, pleased that a difficult moment had passed without too much discomfort.

Mark's cool voice cut across their laughter with a dampening effect. 'And what made you leave Atyimba, Shannon?' he asked, his gaze holding hers inflexibly.

Resentment flared within Shannon. It wasn't that she disputed his right to ask the questions, but rather it was his manner she was objecting to. Did he always quiz newcomers so sceptically? As far as she could see there hadn't been a single thing she had said wrong so far to make him suspicious, and certainly there was no reason for him to treat her to such a cold-eyed scrutiny on her first evening. With her head held high, she eyed him back defiantly.

'Oh, I just decided on a change,' she relayed her explanation airily. 'Don't all jackaroos—and jillaroos—get itchy feet after twelve months or so?' she counter-questioned sweetly, knowing herself to be in the right because Guy had been most emphatic on that point.

'Isn't that the truth?' Chris put in with a laugh. 'I know Paul is always saying that some of our jackaroos get the wanderlust more often than the native stockmen.'

'It's occupational therapy, isn't it, Shannon?' Pete sided

with her defensively. 'To work for a year or so on one
station, then move on. Gives you a look at the country and
a wider scope of techniques.'

'That's right,' she nodded agreeably, quite happy to
endorse Pete's understanding of jackaroos' movements.

While Chris and Pete had been talking Mark's eyes had
dropped to his plate, but now his dark head lifted once
more and his tawny eyes, penetratingly alert, trained on
Shannon's flushed face again as he questioned, 'I believe
they use horses a great deal up there?' in a deceptively light
voice.

Immediately Shannon became wary and berated herself
ruthlessly for allowing her gaze to fall before his as she
faltered, 'Er—yes, they do.'

'So you would be a proficient rider by now?' with a half-
smile curving his lips which Shannon could only call mocking, and which had the effect of dispelling her weariness
and replacing it with a surge of temper.

In a burst of bravado she forced herself to hold his glance
challengingly this time and retorted swiftly, 'I wouldn't call
myself an expert, Mr Seymour, but I think I'm reasonable.'

Well, she shrugged philosophically, she was sure she
would be if she had ever had the chance to learn. And just
maybe a decisive answer would put him off the track better
than one offered in a less assertive manner. Unfortunately,
it did nothing of the kind, as his next words proved.

'Good,' he commended with a sardonic inclination of his
dark head. 'Then you'll be able to accompany me tomorrow
and we can take a look over the place together.' And he
smiled for the first time that evening.

But it was a smile that had Shannon's stomach halting in
mid-plummet on its way to her feet where his disquieting
words had first sent it, and starting to perform in an entirely different way when she realised just how attractive
Mark Seymour could be. With an effort she tore her eyes
away and compelled herself to pay attention to what was

being said by the others at the table.

Mrs Seymour was the first to speak. 'You won't mind if I come with you, Mark, will you?' she asked. 'I'd like to complete the set of sketches I made out at the holding yards last week.'

'Not with us, Nola, I'm sorry. We'll be riding,' Mark rejected her suggestion gently but firmly. 'Pete can take you out in the ute instead, if you like.'

'All right,' his stepmother accepted the change easily, returning to her meal as Pete eyed his elder brother with a grin.

'I thought you said you'd be checking over the entrants for the show with Jim tomorrow,' he accused banteringly. 'I was planning to take Shannon round the property.'

Mark received his brother's look evenly. 'Sorry to disappoint you, Pete, but I've changed my mind. There's nothing urgent that Jim can't handle on his own, and I think Shannon's initiation as to how we do things on Tuesday should come from me,' he justified his decision smoothly.

'I might have known,' muttered Pete good-naturedly beneath his breath, sending a wink in Shannon's direction.

Whatever the reason for Mark Seymour's change of plans, Shannon was certain that Pete's apparent interpretation was very wide of the mark. His stepbrother might not be 'averse to having a pretty face around' as Pete had stated earlier in the day, but she had the distinct impression that, for some particular reason known only to himself, Mark was extremely suspicious of her, and the thought of him showing her over the property because he wanted her company was nothing short of absurd. She had the uneasy feeling it was for an entirely different reason that he had decided she was to partner him on this first tour of inspection.

Although by now her appetite had completely disappeared, Shannon was relieved that the remainder of the mealtime was occupied by less perturbing subjects of conversation, and not long after the dishes had been washed and put away and the children safely tucked into bed, she used the excuse that she hadn't slept very well on the train the night before as the reason for an early escape from her employer's alert presence—but not before Pete had unknowingly managed to cause her a few more anxious moments.

'Going to write up your daily record?' he called after her with a smile as she headed for the hallway.

Shannon stopped and turned back to face him, all too conscious of Mark's watchful look from the corner of her eye. 'My daily record?' she frowned.

'Didn't you have to keep one at Atyimba?' He sounded extremely surprised. 'Wherever I've jackarooed it's always been *suggested*,' with heavy accent, 'that we keep a diary of the work carried out each day, etcetera. We always used to do ours immediately after dinner so we could get it out of the way as soon as possible,' he added with wry feeling.

'Oh, that!' Shannon made herself laugh lightly. 'Yes, well, I expect I shall soon get back into routine. I—I seem to have lost the habit of keeping records since being back in Sydney,' she hoped she had explained her confusion away with a smile.

Once safely in her bedroom she walked quickly over to the writing table and lit a cigarette with fingers that were a little unsteady, drawing on it deeply in an effort to control the nervous fluctuations of her pulse rate. This was going to be worse than even she had imagined! At almost every turn she was demonstrating her ignorance—showing unfamiliarity and incomprehension where there should have been immediate recognition and experience. How she was coming to hate that word 'experience'!

She paced restlessly across the room in front of the bookshelves and, as an idea suddenly sprang into her mind, sank down on to her haunches and diligently checked through the volumes resting there. A few minutes later she rose despairingly upright again and pulled a disgruntled face at the blameless literature. You'd think they would have at least *one* reference book on riding, she criticised sarcastically. Or was it supposed to be a natural accomplishment immediately one set foot over the Dividing Range? She was going riding tomorrow and, with rising panic at the thought, she hadn't got the faintest idea what to do! Oh, curse her reunion with Guy Crawford! Right at that moment she would willingly settle for a politely worded refusal to any application she might have sent in for the post.

CHAPTER THREE

IT was with no small feelings of trepidation the following morning that Shannon dressed in a new pink and white checked shirt, belted navy blue denims about her slim waist, pushed her feet into unfamiliar stock boots and dragged a heavy sweater over her head as protection against the early morning chill. Already she could hear the children chattering to Chris in the kitchen and reluctantly deciding she could put off the hour of reckoning no longer stepped through the doorway with her shoulders squared and her head held high.

'All set and ready to go, I see,' commented Chris on her appearance with a smile when Shannon walked into the kitchen. 'I usually feed these two first,' she explained, nodding to where Jane and Davey, perched on long-legged stools beside the breakfast bar, were rapidly consuming the last morsels of their morning cereal, as she began ladling sausages and eggs on to two plates. 'Then they can tidy their room and get everything ready for school while we're having ours.'

'Anything I can do to help, Chris?' Shannon asked when the older girl had finished serving Jane and Davey.

'You can get me a dozen eggs from the fridge, as well as Mark and Pete's steaks if you would, please, Shannon. Get one for yourself too if you'd like one, there's no shortage of meat here,' she grinned. 'The men should be back soon and, in fact, Tony's here already with the milk. He *is* early this morning,' she remarked in surprise as a tall figure passed the window and a knock sounded on the kitchen door.

The blond jackaroo whose windbreaker was buttoned tightly against the elements and whose twinkling blue eyes ranged over the four occupants of the room with his cheery, 'Morning, all,' as he handed over a bucket of warm milk that steamed in the cold air, swept his bush hat from his head with a flourish upon Chris's smiling introduction to their newest employee.

'Glad to meet you, Shannon,' he returned in unabashed admiration. 'You coming out on the property with us to-day?'

'No, she's going out with Mark,' Chris laughingly supplied the information which brought a crestfallen look to his face. 'Give her a chance, Tony, she hasn't been here twenty-four hours yet. There'll be plenty of time for you to get acquainted with Shannon in the weeks to come.'

'I'll look forward to it,' he grinned irrepressibly in answer, clapping his hat back on to his head firmly and raising a hand in friendly salute before closing the door behind him.

Apart from a few requests to be allowed to take treasured possessions with them to school, which received affirmative replies from Chris, the children finished their breakfasts quietly and headed for the bathroom while their mother and Shannon completed the preparations for the rest of the meal.

The next blast of cold air from the opening door preceded Mark's arrival as he slung a sheepskin jacket on to the straight-backed settle by the door to reveal a denim shirt and moleskin pants, and stood with hands thrust deep into his back pockets and his feet slightly apart.

The head-to-toe appraisal she received from enigmatic eyes after a rather abrupt greeting had Shannon's indignation flaring uncontrollably and she found herself staring back at him in a belligerent manner which, she conceded wryly, was not normally reserved for one's employer. But then his wasn't the normal conduct meted out to an employee either, she excused herself righteously, and continued to hold that steady gaze unblinkingly until his lips curved sardonically and, in confusion, she swung her eyes away.

Softly spoken words drawled slowly across the room. 'They must have worked you hard in Queensland,' he said.

Shannon's eyes lifted once more and she looked at him puzzledly. 'What makes you say that?' she queried warily, fingers curling nervously at her sides.

One eyebrow rose in succinct irony. 'You needed all new gear,' he replied pointedly.

Damn! Why hadn't she thought to scuff her boots a little and wash some of the newness from her clothes before leaving Sydney? Hastily she concentrated on what Chris was doing in the dining room lest her discomfiture should become too noticeable and with a shaky laugh dissembled, 'New job—new clothes,' with defensively hunched shoulders. 'What's wrong with that?'

'Nothing that I know of—how about you?' he reversed the question coolly.

'I—I don't know what—what you mean,' she stammered, feeling the telltale heat rising in her cheeks. 'I needed new clothes, so I bought them. I didn't think anyone would make a federal case out of it. Or aren't jillaroos supposed to wear anything new around here?' she concluded with protective sarcasm.

'Okay, have it your way,' Mark shrugged, indifferently almost. 'But just remember ... I don't take kindly to being crossed, so think twice before you commit yourself to something you can't handle,' he warned grimly, and strode past her without so much as a sideways glance.

Shannon swallowed hard and wished herself miles away. Attractive he might be, but there was also a hint of ruthlessness about Mark Seymour that couldn't be ignored and which didn't augur well for her first outing in his company.

'Think twice before you commit yourself,' he had said. Well, it was too late for that now. She *had* committed herself three weeks ago when she allowed Mr Crawford to believe the story Guy had invented, and her reasons for not telling the truth then still held good to her mind. She had no intention of causing trouble for Guy—either with his father, or with Mark Seymour!

Still, she attempted to view the matter in a more optimistic light, perhaps she was making things out to be a lot worse than they actually were. Quite often it was possible to build matters up in one's own mind to proportions they just didn't possess when the problem was faced squarely. She expelled a deeply held breath and turned back to the eggs she had been breaking into the frying pan, determined to put her best foot forward and leave the rest to fate.

Breakfast was over by seven-thirty and once Mrs Seymour and Pete had disappeared to her studio to collect her sketch book and drawing implements, Mark rose leisurely to his feet and moved into the kitchen with an agile tread.

'I'll be with you in a minute, Shannon,' he said. 'In the meantime though, you can saddle up the piebald mare for yourself at the stables.'

'But you...' Chris began with a frown, only to be silenced when her brother held up an imperious hand, his expression totally unreadable as he advised evenly,

'I know what I'm doing, Chris. I think the mare will be quite suitable for Shannon's use.'

Chris subsided with an oblique moue and Shannon looked perplexedly from one to the other before shrugging her shoulders dismissively, collecting her jacket from the bedroom, and heading down the verandah steps. She had more than enough on her mind at the moment to be worrying over family differences of opinion—they could sort that out for themselves.

First, and by no means least, was the question as to whether one could actually ride a horse without having been taught beforehand. She had never been frightened of animals and hoped this would give her some slight advantage in the 'deception stakes' as she was coming to think of it. If she looked too uncomfortable in the saddle she could always say ... what? That she was out of practice? No, that wouldn't do. Her mind tumbled onwards feverishly. Ah, that was more like it! She could tell him she had taken a bad fall the last time she had been riding and hadn't quite got her nerve back yet. Yes, that would have to do ... unless, of course, she could come up with something more plausible in the meantime.

Marching into the stone-flagged stables, she grimaced as her untrained eye ran over the four horses left in their stalls. Now all she had to do was find the right mount. From some dim recollection she had the feeling piebald was a mixture of colours, and with this thought in mind she began a closer inspection of the waiting animals. The first two she discarded immediately—one was brown, the other chestnut—but the next two had her sighing despondently. Which was the piebald? The slightly smaller horse was a sort of chestnut colour thickly interspersed with blotches and streaks of white, while the other was a beautiful creamy tan colour with white markings on its face and legs, and bearing a white mane and tail.

Mentally Shannon tossed up between the two of them,

chose the smaller, and her decision made, began looking
about her for a bridle. This much she had gleaned from
watching movies and television. Finding one with the reins
already attached proved to be easy, but getting the bit into
the mare's mouth was something else again and caused her
to wonder if it was a case of the horse sensing she was
nervously unfamiliar and playing up because of it, but at
last she succeeded in getting it over the lower teeth and
hurried to buckle the cheek strap before anything else could
happen. The animal led willingly out of its straw-lined stall
but, once outside, immediately began to dance and stamp
skittishly, hooves ringing on the stone floor and a playful
head pushing into Shannon's shoulder when she attempted
to tether the reins to a ring-bolt beside the stable door.

'Not saddled yet?'

The words spoken in a mocking drawl had her whirling
around to see Mark leaning negligently against the furthest
stable door, dressed once more in his sheepskin jacket, hat
sitting well forward on his forehead. How long he had been
there she didn't know—she could only hope he hadn't witnessed too much of her slow and unsure handling of the
horse still tending to prance at the end of her reins.

With a shake of her head she replied with all the nonchalance she could muster, 'Not yet, I'm sorry, although I
shouldn't be long now,' hoping Mark would begin saddling
his own mount so that she could covertly watch and follow
suit.

'Doesn't matter.' He flexed wide shoulders impassively
and moved towards her with a casual stride. 'I've changed
my mind—we'll take the four-wheel drive instead. You *can*
drive?'

The question flicked out with the sharp sting of a whip as
he took the reins from her unresisting fingers and led the
mare back into her stall while Shannon's thoughts came to a
standstill. No, even she wasn't naïve enough to think she
could bluff her way through that! So when he bolted the

stable door and returned the bridle to its appropriate hook a moment later, his brows still raised in silent interrogation, it was to find Shannon facing him staunchly.

'No, I can't drive, Mr Seymour,' she admitted truthfully. 'There—there wasn't time for anybody to teach me last year,' not quite so truthfully.

Another imperturbable movement of his shoulders followed, but the accompanying, 'You don't surprise me,' was anything but unconcerned and Shannon had to bite her tongue in an effort not to pursue his obscure statement further, somehow certain that if she did so she would only be giving him yet another opportunity to dispute her qualifications. In lieu, she attempted to give a knowledgeable smile, but this was so pointedly ignored when Mark turned on his heel and strode for the door in such long-legged determination that Shannon, her face flaming and her temper seething at his deliberate snub, had no option but to break into an undignified trot in order to keep pace with him.

The wind sweeping across the landscape, causing the trees to lean and sway majestically and the grass to bow down in rippling waves of green as the Land Rover cut its way over open paddocks and wooded slopes, cooled Shannon's cheeks and temper, but long before they had reached their destination it had penetrated her clothing to the extent that she was forced to hug her jacket closer to her slender form and fold her arms across her midriff so that she could tuck her exposed hands within the superficial warmth.

'Is that the heaviest coat you own?' Mark suddenly sent her a sharp look of exasperation tinged with impatience.

Shannon intercepted his glance balefully. What business was it of his what she wore? The expenses incurred by her father's illness had precluded any more expensive covering—especially one of the type he was wearing so inconsequentially.

'It will do,' she retorted brashly. 'It will be warmer in an hour or so,' her hopeful eyes turned skyward to where the sun was hiding behind a white streak of cloud, 'and a little bit of cold doesn't bother *me*,' with meaningful sarcasm as she allowed her eyes to slide over the length of sheepskin only inches away from her arm.

In turn his eyes halted significantly for a second on the arms that were folded about her so protectively and his lip curled sardonically.

'Just as well, otherwise you *would* be in a bad way, wouldn't you?' he mocked.

'Don't worry, Mr Seymour, it won't affect my capabilities as a jillaroo,' she returned hotly.

'Oh, I never thought it would,' he replied softly—so amiably in fact that Shannon immediately suspected some ulterior meaning and waited apprehensively for him to continue. But when he did, his words came as a complete surprise.

'What do your parents feel about you jillarooing, Shannon? Don't they mind you being away from home for long periods at a time?' he asked.

For a time all Shannon could do was to stare at him blankly, so unexpected had been the questions, but then she bit at her lip and tore her gaze away to concentrate unseeingly on the sheep they were passing.

'I wouldn't know ... they're both dead,' she finally divulged woodenly, reluctantly, wanting only to nurse her grief to herself.

'So you're alone in the world?'

If that was the beginning of pity she could detect in his voice, Shannon didn't want any of it, and she tilted her head disdainfully.

'I prefer to think of it as being a free agent, going where I please and owing allegiance to no one but myself,' she retorted, trying to make it obvious she considered it was none of his concern.

'A rather selfish outlook, wouldn't you say?'

'Perhaps,' she shrugged indifferently. She hadn't intended that it should sound that way, but she wasn't all that interested in putting forth any lengthy explanations either. Let him think what he liked! She was too aware that she would soon have other matters to worry her now they had begun making their way towards a set of wooden yards in the near distance where the red- and white-coated cattle were churning up clouds of dust as they protested both vocally and physically at the curtailment of their freedom.

'I don't suppose you brought a sharp knife with you?' Mark now asked abruptly as the vehicle started to slow.

Shannon's brows arched expressively. 'Was I supposed to?'

A tiny muscle pulled at the corner of his mouth and tawny eyes raked over her bleakly. 'Perhaps not,' he conceded heavily, but immediately carried on, 'You do have a notebook and pencil with you, though?'

Shannon wasn't about to be impaled by one of those ruthless looks again and she lied swiftly, 'Yes, I have them here,' plunging an icy hand into the back pocket of her jeans and pulling a suitably dismayed face when it came out empty. 'Oh, dear, they must have fallen out when I was saddling the horse,' she lamented hollowly.

Mark ground the vehicle to a savage halt beside the yards which had been erected beneath the intertwining branches of a clump of yellow box trees, almost throwing Shannon into the windscreen as he did so, and grated, 'I should have bloody well guessed!' in infuriated tones as he swung his long length out of his seat.

Wincing at the slam of the door when it closed, Shannon hesitantly alighted from her own side to stand staring at the amount of activity taking place within the wooden enclosure.

'Here!' Mark called to her across the bonnet of the Land Rover, and tossed something to her which she only just managed to catch in cold fingers after turning to look at him enquiringly. She found herself holding an expensive leather-covered notebook with a small gold pencil inserted in its appropriate niche. 'You can use mine for today. Just make sure you don't lose that one too, eh?' he called again in undisguised satire and, unchaining the gate, let himself into the yard.

With the notebook pushed deep into her pocket, Shannon stood shivering indecisively where he had left her, totally unsure of her surroundings and wholly unconscious that her bewilderment was visible. How could Guy have thought she would be able to bluff her way through all this? she sighed despairingly.

'We haven't got all day! Get yourself down here!'

Mark's impatient roar had her suddenly jumping into nervous action, pushing in past the gate and making her way unenthusiastically to his side, whereupon he gibed, 'No wonder you find it easy to forget. Do you always stand that far away when you're being taught something?'

A rosy stain of colour mounted Shannon's cheeks and she licked at her lips apprehensively. 'I wasn't sure if you . . . if I . . .' she began with a doubtful movement of her hands.

'As far as I can see, you're never sure about anything,' he interrupted callously, and ran an exasperated hand around the back of his neck. 'Anyway, I guess you'd better meet the rest of the men while you're here,' he went on in a more resigned tone, which had Shannon letting out a relieved breath. It was bad enough just having him around, without his baiting her all the time as well.

The introductions completed, Mark continued talking with his overseer while Shannon watched dubiously as Tony, the jackaroo she had met earlier that morning, and Rex Tatnell, one of the stockmen, proceeded with their branding of the small but vigorous young calves. A firm hand gripping her shoulder had her swinging around warily as Mark nodded towards the two men.

'If one of them keeps the race full and the other operates

the crush while you brand, they'll finish in half the time,' he suggested logically, but luckily had turned back to continue his discussion with Wade Reardon before Shannon's feeling of sheer horror at the proposal actually registered on her face.

Correctly surmising there would be no chance of a reprieve when it was clearly assumed she would know what to do, she crossed the yard with reluctant and faltering steps to where the men were working and stood hovering by the fire as they released one branded calf and replaced it with another.

'Ready when you are, Shannon,' Tony called over his shoulder from his position beside the race and, with a sinking heart, she gingerly extracted one of the long-handled irons from the fire and walked towards them.

Slowly she angled the iron between the rails and closer to the slightly curly hide in front of her as she had seen them doing, but was abruptly halted by Tony's appalled, 'Not that low, Shannon! Up here!' as he slapped one hand above the animal's hip.

'Sorry,' she murmured hoarsely, biting at her lip with concentration, and tried again, but this time thrusting the iron forward determinedly and almost closing her eyes in distaste when it finally made contact with the hair.

'Hell, Shannon! Don't roast the poor little blighter! The boss'll skin you alive if he finds you doing that to any of his stud cattle.'

The reference to Mark, as much as Tony's expostulation on behalf of the animal, had her wide-eyed once more and she rapidly withdrew the offending iron with a plaintive, 'Oh, help! I hope I didn't hurt him too much.'

'Don't worry, he'll survive,' he calmed her fears with a grin, and daubed the calf generously with Stockholm tar before setting it free.

So apprehensive was she of doing the same thing again that it took three attempts before she had managed to put a reasonably distinguishable mark on the next sufferer, and turning to replace the iron in the fire she found Mark observing her actions silently, long fingers resting lightly on slim hips and an unfathomable expression on his face as the calf with the distorted brand sped past in front of him.

Quickly she dragged her gaze away and resolutely withdrew the iron from the fire as soon as Tony had another one ready for her and, with him whispering helpful instructions, this time managed to brand the animal almost legibly without blistering its hide too much in the process.

And that provided the routine for the next hour or more, although Shannon was positive she could have achieved far more satisfactory results had she not had to perform the task under Mark's ever-watchful eye. She was conscious of his presence the whole time and, consequently, found herself fumbling on many occasions when she was sure that, had he not been there, she could have produced far more pleasing results.

As it was she still continued to burn some and blotched others, while only a very small percentage of those she attended to were fortunate enough to escape with a reasonable identification singed on to their coats. She had even managed to scorch her own fingers by grabbing the iron too near the heated end when, because she had been too busy looking to see if Mark was still observing them so carefully, she had tripped and come close to branding Tony instead.

By the time the billy had been boiled for morning tea Shannon didn't need the sun to warm her, she had generated enough nervous heat of her own and had already stripped off her jacket and sweater, and rolled the sleeves of her shirt up past her elbows. Sitting back against the stockyard rails with her knees drawn up before her, she gratefully accepted a mug of steaming black tea from Tony's outstretched hand and wiped the back of one wrist across her slightly perspiring forehead, wishing she had thought to bring her cigarettes along. She could certainly do with one right now!

Perhaps Tony was a mind-reader, for no sooner had the idea entered Shannon's head than he lowered himself to the ground beside her and held out a flip-top box.

'Want one?' he smiled sympathetically.

Shannon pulled an expressive face. 'Do I ever! Thanks, Tony,' she returned with feeling, and drew deeply on the cigarette once he had put a match to it. 'I made a complete shambles of it, didn't I?' she grimaced, nodding to where the rest of the calves continued to mill in the yard.

Tony pushed his hat further forward to shade his eyes and shrugged fatalistically. 'Well, I wouldn't exactly say you were the best I'd ever seen,' he grinned. 'How's the hand, anyway?'

A glance at her fingers disclosed skin that was still red and somewhat puffy. 'It'll be okay. At least the skin isn't broken,' she dismissed the painful area casually. 'Maybe it was poetic justice for what I was putting those calves through,' she half-laughed in self-mockery.

Tony's eyes scanned the small herd intently. 'Yes, well, it could look as if some doubtful poddy-dodging's been going on,' he remarked judiciously. 'Maybe it's as well the boss is known around these parts.'

'You mean people still steal cattle? In this day and age?'

'Sure they do,' he confirmed positively. 'Although I would have thought you'd know that from having worked in Queensland. I've always been led to believe it's more prevalent up there than it is in New South Wales.'

Oh, curses, she'd put her foot in it again! But in order to keep up the pretence she took a mouthful of tea, shook her head and assured him in properly impressive tones, 'Not around where I was.'

For a few minutes they smoked and drank their tea in companionable silence, listening to the sounds of nature— the cattle bellowing less often now as they submitted resignedly to their temporary captivity, the two birds in the box tree above them squabbling stridently over a particularly choice morsel of food, and the shushing of the grass and leaves as they bent beneath the stirring wind.

Suddenly a long shadow was cast over the two of them and Shannon raised deep blue eyes to find Mark looking down on them expressionlessly. A rueful smile pulled at Tony's mouth, as with a reluctant sigh, he dropped his cigarette butt on the ground, poured the remains of his tea over it as an extinguisher, and heaved himself to his feet. Not wanting to appear lacking in enthusiasm for her work, Shannon swiftly followed suit, but when she would have followed Tony back to the fire a hard hand around her upper arm halted her and she waited suspensefully for some cutting remark to be made regarding her efforts of the morning.

To her utter amazement none were forthcoming. 'No, we'll be moving on now, Shannon,' was all Mark said, and called over his shoulder to his overseer as he shepherded her through the gate, 'We'll see you later this afternoon, Wade,' which was acknowledged by one tanned hand reaching to the battered brim of that man's hat.

Lunchtime came and went in a panic-stricken blur for Shannon, shiveringly aware as she was of Mark's vigilant glances and the almost palpable feeling of turbulent exacerbation kept under control only by the strongest self-discipline that emanated from his tautly held frame and evidenced by the explosive movement of a muscle in the increasingly aggressive set of his jaw.

If he had recently made some comment—criticised, complained, or even derided—Shannon might have felt better, but his silence had her going from bad to worse as the day wore on and the tension within herself had intensified with every mistake she made until she was a quivering mass of frayed confidence and gauche ability.

During her attempts at drenching a yard of mustered

sheep her fingers had been chewed, bitten and grazed; her feet trodden on and her ankles and shins kicked numerous times, and she was certain there was more of the liquid covering her clothes than ever she had managed to pump down their throats, and although Mark might not have made any remarks upon her awkwardness, he had still kept up his periodic interrogations during the afternoon and the more questions he asked the more hesitant and groping became her replies until his last cool, 'What sort of programme did they have on Atyimba for the eradication of noxious weeds?' had her shoulders sagging in defeated hopelessness and whispering, 'I—I can't remember,' in a shaking voice.

Still he said nothing, only that determined chin thrusting forward a shade more uncompromisingly and an expression of scornful disbelief flashing across his face as an indication of what he might be thinking when, for the second time that day, he led the way from the Land Rover down to the yards where Shannon had received such a disastrous initiation into branding.

This time, however, she followed him beyond the gate without waiting for a sardonic summons and smiled faintly in response to Tony's wink when he stopped beside her while Mark spoke to his overseer.

'What happened to you?' he eyed her generously bespattered jeans and shirt with a grin. 'Dropped the drench container, did you?'

'Actually . . . no.' Shannon gave a self-conscious laugh in return. 'It just looks that way.'

'Nervous on your first day with a new employer, eh?'

A swift glance towards Mark and she nodded emphatically. 'You could say that,' she conceded with an eloquent raising of her brows.

'Never mind, I expect you'll find it easier tomorrow.'

'I certainly hope so,' Shannon agreed wholeheartedly. 'I don't think I could stand another one like today.'

'I doubt the stock could either!' put in a satirical voice close beside her ear, bringing a deep flush of humiliation to scald her cheeks and Tony to suppress his laughter with difficulty. 'How's the ear-tagging coming along, Tony?' Mark now asked. 'Nearly finished?'

'Sure thing, boss,' the jackaroo replied with a trace of a grin still hovering at the corners of his mouth. 'Another hour will see us through.'

Mark accepted the information with a nod. 'Good work,' he said, and turned to Shannon as Tony headed back towards the cattle race. 'Done any tagging before?' he queried evenly.

Shannon swallowed her dismay and refused to meet his gaze. 'No—er—yes—er . . .' she started to stammer.

'And just what's that supposed to mean?' came the stony interruption. 'Surely you know whether you have or you haven't!'

Never had Shannon known a day to seem longer and her brain wasn't working as clearly, or as quickly, as it might have done. Now all she could do was to stare dejectedly at the ground and shrug, 'Yes, well, I've—um—I've seen it done, but I've—er—I've never done any myself. I—er just meant . . .'

'*Right!*'

The word seemed to burst uncontrollably from Mark's tightly drawn lips as it sliced through her stuttered explanation before steely fingers wrapped themselves about her arm, bringing a look of worried consternation to her blue eyes as they sought his face when she was propelled at a stumble-footed pace out of the yards and up to the Land Rover.

'Get in, you curly-headed little liar!' she was ordered in stark inflexible tones, his fingers biting deeper into her soft flesh to enforce the command. 'You and I are about to set the record straight!'

If she hadn't been quite so tired Shannon might have welcomed the idea of her subterfuge being exposed, but at the moment she didn't feel up to defending herself against his overwhelming presence within the close confines of the vehicle and she shook her head negatively.

'I'd rather stand, if you don't mind,' she murmured huskily.

'Well, I do mind,' he returned grimly, sarcastically, and urged her domineeringly into the front passenger seat. 'In fact, there's quite a few aspects of this little fraud of yours that I mind!' he continued with disparaging emphasis after taking his own seat behind the wheel.

'Fraud? I—I don't know what you're talking about! I haven't done anything ... criminal,' Shannon felt she had to protest.

'Haven't you?' he gibed harshly. 'I doubt whether the calves you branded—for want of a better word—would have such a forbearing view! And for your information fraud is defined, among other things, as an act of deceit involving misrepresentation. And that just about says it all, doesn't it? Although what I'm really interested to hear,' he went on in the same implacable voice without waiting for an answer, 'is how you managed to persuade Harry Crawford to write such a glowing letter of introduction for you. Harry's no fool when it comes to hiring staff and I think I'm entitled to that much before I decide what's to be done with you.'

Not for one moment could Shannon deny that he was justified in expecting an explanation, but at the same time she couldn't deliberately divulge Guy's participation in the scheme either, so she merely breathed a tremulous, 'I'm sorry, Mr Seymour,' and hugged her crumpled jacket to her stomach in an effort to stop herself from shaking with unwanted nerves.

'Is that *all*?'

Her eyes strayed tentatively to his and away again immediately she saw the unyielding look in them and she moved her hands evocatively.

'What more can I say? I wanted to become a jillaroo and there were no advertisements for anyone without experience,' she confessed shamefacedly.

'So I was to be the poor fool with the unenviable task of teaching you, is that it?' he snapped angrily.

'Some—something like that,' she had to admit, but unwillingly, not liking his chosen turn of phrase but unable to disabuse him of the sentiments expressed.

Amber eyes raked over her coldly as his hand searched for cigarettes and lighter in the pocket of his shirt.

'Well, there might be some things I wouldn't mind teaching you, Miss Marshall, but jillarooing's not one of them,' he ground out succinctly. 'And you still haven't explained how you convinced Harry you'd done this type of work before. Did you send someone else along in your place for the interview?' he guessed contemptuously, and drew sharply on his cigarette.

Shannon gazed longingly at the white cylinder held between tanned fingers then shook her head in repudiation and looked blindly out at the stockyards.

'No,' she rejected his assumption miserably.

'No ... what?'

'No, Mr Seymour,' she deliberately misunderstood him, stalling for time and futilely hoping he would tire of noncommittal answers.

'That wasn't what I meant, and you know it!' he ignored her stratagem. Then, 'Damn you, Shannon, look at me when I'm talking to you!' as an ungentle hand sank into her dark curls and forced her head round towards him. 'I want a straight answer from you ... if that's possible! I want to know how you managed to get past Harry Crawford and, by God, I'm going to find out ... even if I have to ring him myself and tell him the whole story!'

'Oh, no, please don't do that!' She lifted unconsciously pleading eyes to his involuntarily, knowing how such an action would disclose their irresponsibility to Guy's parent.

'Then you'd better start talking, hadn't you?' he suggested remorsely.

She bit at her lip worriedly and gave her head an imperceptible shake. 'I'm sorry, Mr Seymour ... but I can't.'

'Can't ... or won't?' he demanded adamantly.

She hunched her shoulders on a defeated sigh. 'Either way, the result's the same, isn't it?'

As if losing interest Mark now removed his hand from her hair and leant back against the door of the vehicle, half turning in his seat as he did so.

'You don't happen to know *Guy* Crawford, do you?' he enquired almost casually, although there was nothing casual about his narrowed and alert eyes.

The need for Shannon to answer aloud didn't arise. The steady invasion of colour into her cheeks made it completely unnecessary, and the implications of that deep flush weren't lost on her interrogator either, for his lip curled sardonically and his head nodded slowly in silent confirmation.

'So now we come to the truth of it, eh?' he jeered. 'Whimsical Guy decides to put in a good word for his current girl-friend so she can get the job she wants, but isn't qualified for. How extremely chivalrous of him! Although I can't help but wonder just how you were kind enough to reward him for all his trouble,' with derisive insinuation.

'How dare you!' Shannon gasped in wide-eyed shock. Up until then she had been prepared to suffer his anger and scorn in dismal acceptance, knowing him to have right on his side, but now he had gone too far, and she had no intention of letting such a denigrating remark pass unchallenged and her natural ebullience began to reassert itself as she rounded on him indignantly. 'How dare you suggest that I—that I...'

' "Slept" is the word you're looking for, I believe,' he interposed mockingly.

'Well, I didn't!' she flashed at him, her eyes sparkling like two dark sapphires. 'Guy's not like that!' And in retaliation for one raised and dissentient eyebrow, 'No, he's not! He's a friend, that's all!'

'And one with whom you'll be pleased to renew acquaintace, I gather.'

'Y-e-es,' warily.

'That's good, because when he meets your train you can tell him personally that if he ever dares to pull such a stunt on me again, he'll rue the day he was born!' with grim intent.

Shannon stared at him in growing dismay as his words registered. 'Are you ... firing me?' she queried hesitantly.

His head dipped in wry acknowledgment. 'You catch on quick, blue eyes! What did you expect? A promotion?' he enquired sarcastically. 'You can take tomorrow's train back to Sydney.'

'Tomorrow's train!' she echoed, aghast. 'But I can't! I haven't got...' she halted, pride preventing her from letting him know just how low her finances were.

'You haven't got ... what?' he prompted with a frown, then sighed and combed an exasperated hand through his hair. 'The money for your fare?' he supposed correctly.

'It doesn't matter,' she sniffed disdainfully.

'I'm sure Guy would be only too willing to come to your aid.'

Shannon hugged her jacket even tighter. 'I wouldn't presume to ask him,' she mumbled in a low tone.

'No one at all who could help you?' A miserable shake of her head and Mark sighed again. 'Okay, I'll buy the ticket for you,' he said.

'Don't do me any favours, Mr Seymour,' she promptly

fired back at him resentfully. 'Even though you're obviously prepared to go to any lengths to be rid of me, I'd rather walk than accept charity from you!'

'Walk?' He sounded amused. 'What—all seven hundred and ninety kilometres?' in a lazy drawl as he stubbed out his cigarette.

'If I have to!' she blazed irrationally. 'Or I should be able to hitch-hike for most of it.'

Gone was Mark's indolent indifference as Shannon felt him tense beside her and he fixed her with a quelling glance.

'Don't you dare, you irresponsible little fool!' he ordered autocratically and making her flinch from the raw anger shining in his eyes. 'Haven't you got more sense than to come up with an imprudent idea like that?'

'Without any money I don't have much choice, do I?' she challenged with an ironic lifting of her own brows. 'What would you suggest I do under the circumstances ... sprout wings and fly?' in unconcealed insolence.

'For a start, I'd suggest you put a guard on that incautious tongue of yours before it lands you in more trouble than you've already got,' he advised with tight-lipped control.

'Would you? I don't see why,' she defied him flippantly. 'After all, you're not even my boss any more. You just fired me ... remember?'

'How could I forget?' he taunted just as mockingly. 'It's not every day of the week that we have Guy's sleeping partners attempting to pass themselves off as a jillaroo. It's been quite an education.'

The degrading description took Shannon's breath away for a moment, but then all the disappointment of losing her job, the pent-up tension from a day of working under Mark's critical gaze, and the frustration of knowing all her efforts had been in vain anyway suddenly exploded within her and she swung to face him smoulderingly, her breasts heaving with the force of her feelings.

'Well, I only hope *that*'s just as instructive!' she stormed as her open hand slapped against the side of his bronzed face with an intensity that left her palm stinging when she clapped it to her mouth a second later in horrified misgiving at what she had done.

'You little vixen!' he grated savagely between clenched teeth, while Shannon could see all too clearly the reddening inprint of her hand on his skin. 'Now let's see how rough you really want to play, shall we?' and she was hauled unceremoniously across the seat to be brought up hard against an extremely masculine chest.

Frantically Shannon began to struggle, but her wild efforts proved totally inadequate against the overpowering weight of his body as he pinned her to the seat, an inexorable hand tilting her head back relentlessly.

'Mr Seymour ... Mark...!' she attempted to demur apprehensively, but that was as far as she managed to get before his well-shaped mouth covered hers in a kiss that was clearly meant as a reprisal for her own reckless castigation.

CHAPTER FOUR

SHANNON had instinctively known from their very first meeting that Mark Seymour was no novice when it came to the art of making love, and now he was proving her intuitive processes correct as his lips rejected any opposition and demanded a capitulation she had no way of evading. The stimulating pressure of his warm body, combined with the tantalising mastery of his mouth, was making her heart pound crazily and the blood to beat deafeningly in her ears, but still he showed no sign of releasing her. Not until her soft lips parted provocatively and responded with an unconditional fervour to his compelling dominance did he finally raise his head and dismissively thrust her back into her own seat.

'I wouldn't advise you to try something like that again, Shannon, or you might not get off so lightly,' he warned with cool self-assurance, leaning forward to switch on the ignition.

Bemused and shaken by the strength of her wayward emotions, Shannon could only stare unseeingly through the dusty windscreen while the remembrance of his callous rebuff of her uninhibited reaction curled humiliatingly through her insides. He called what she had just experienced 'getting off lightly' did he? After he had deliberately ploughed every particle of her pride and self-respect into the ground and brought to the surface an unsuspected but deeply passionate side of her nature?

Falteringly her fingers explored the curving contours of her lips where the explosiveness of Mark's touch still lingered and hot tears of reaction began to spill on to her lashes which were brushed away impatiently with the back of one hand. Whatever happened she couldn't allow him to guess just how devastating his punishing kiss had been.

'Stop feeling so sorry for yourself,' Mark's voice roughly interrupted her unsettled thoughts. 'When you slap a man's face you're inviting one of two things—either to be kissed or slapped in return. I think you reaped the more acceptable of the two.'

Shannon wasn't so sure. She was positive that a slap couldn't possibly have caused more discomfort and humiliation than she was already suffering, and spared him only a haughty glance before turning her head away. Let him believe she was feeling sorry for herself because he had kissed her! Rather that than have him know it was her own emotional response which was creating all her heart-burning.

The rest of the journey back to the homestead was accomplished in a tension-filled silence and as soon as Mark halted the vehicle in front of the garage Shannon hastily gathered up her crumpled jacket and sweater, put her legs to the ground and hurried up the slope to the homestead.

'Hi! How did it go today?' Chris greeted her gaily a moment later.

The tears that she had managed to keep at bay on the way home threatened again and Shannon blinked them back furiously.

'I was fired,' she confided throatily.

'Oh, no!' Chris came towards her and laid a consoling arm around her shoulders. 'Whatever for?'

What was the use of prevaricating? 'Because your brother found out I'm not experienced like I claimed to be, and I...' she looked down at her stained clothing and hiccuped ruefully, 'I made complete chaos out of every solitary thing I tried.'

'Not forgetting the fact that Shannon apparently doesn't know the difference between the sexes in the animal world either,' a drawling voice informed them sardonically.

Two heads turned in unison to where Mark's broad frame filled the doorway, a look of frowning incomprehension on Chris's face and one of attempted recollection on Shannon's.

'The horse you were attempting to saddle this morning,' he obligingly reminded her. 'It happens to have been a roan gelding ... not a piebald mare!'

Shannon crimsoned. It had never occurred to her to check, so anxious had she been to select the right colouring, even though that too, apparently, had been incorrect.

'Can you ride, by the way?' Mark now enquired indolently.

Even white teeth bit at a soft underlip as Shannon shook

her head. 'No, I can't,' she admitted with a sigh, refusing to meet his gaze and keeping her eyes on some point between his feet instead.

'But you were going to pretend that you could?' Chris broke in incredulously, and after Shannon's reluctantly nodded confirmation, 'Well, no one could say you weren't game, could they?' she grinned admiringly.

'I could,' her brother stifled her approval coldly. 'I'd be more inclined to call it the height of stupidity! You could have broken your damned fool neck!' he snapped at Shannon.

'Which, I don't doubt, would have pleased you no end!' she retorted swiftly, her fighting spirit coming to the fore and her chin lifting militantly. 'Look what an opportunity you missed by changing your mind and taking the four-wheel drive instead.'

'You think so? You really think I made that decision on a whim—for no particular reason at all?'

Shannon faced him resolutely. 'I don't see why not.'

'Don't you? Not even after watching you tossing up between a roan and a palomino and then taking the best part of ten minutes just to get a bridle on?'

'You mean you guessed *then* that I hadn't done any jillarooing before?' she accused with a gasp.

A short nod and a gibing, 'Now you're getting the picture.'

'But—but why did you—why didn't you . . .?'

'Why didn't I confront you with it? Because I was interested to see just how far you were prepared to go with your little charade, and to confirm the suspicions I'd had from the very minute I set eyes on you.'

'But . . . why?' Shannon couldn't help asking bewilderedly.

'Because you looked as guilty as hell when Chris first introduced us, and . . .' he strode towards her purposefully, making Shannon back nervously away until a cupboard stopped her retreat and Mark's lip curved derisively at her action as he caught hold of one of her hands and held it, palm uppermost, in front of her, 'your hand was as soft and smooth as velvet! I didn't need to be a genius to work out that I was being taken for a ride, blue eyes!' He dropped her hand disgustedly.

A slightly hysterical laugh rose in Shannon's throat. It was the first time in her life that she had encountered someone who could pay compliments and, in the same breath, make them sound like a crime. So she had given herself away from the very beginning! In a way she could even find it in her heart to be a little glad. It had been the first time she had attempted something, she didn't quibble over the word—dishonest—and the relief of knowing it was all over compensated in some small measure for finding herself so precipitately out of work.

But of one thing she was sure, she didn't intend to give Mark Seymour the pleasure of seeing her leave the property wet-eyed and with her proverbial tail between her legs, so she held his cold gaze defiantly and made an insouciant movement with one shoulder.

'As you feel so strongly about it, perhaps you'd also like me to repay you for my board and lodgings too,' she suggested insolently.

'I thought you had no money,' he returned softly, ominously.

'I haven't,' Shannon made herself smile uncaringly at him. 'But I wouldn't want you to think I owed you anything for today's invaluable tuition. After all, that was the arrangement for the original jackaroos in this country, wasn't it? For them to pay the pastoralists to teach them how to run a station? I could give you an I.O.U. and send you the money once I'm employed again, if you like,' she offered with a provocative look.

The muscles along Mark's jaw tightened visibly. 'The only thing I'd like from you, blue eyes, is a view of your back as you leave,' he ground out implicitly. 'And for your sake, the sooner the better, before I give in to the almost uncontrollable desire to break your damned neck personally!'

'Mark!' His name burst from Chris's lips in protest. 'How could you say such a thing?' she remonstrated in a shocked voice.

'Quite easily,' he ignored the rebuke unrepentantly. 'Especially when dealing with a deceitful little cat who, together with her latest flame, deliberately sets out to defraud a good friend of mine, as well as myself, into believing she's a competent jillaroo. That is what you intended, isn't it, Shannon?' he probed mercilessly.

Miserably aware of Chris's eyes turned towards her, it was all Shannon could do not to let fall scalding tears of remorse for her ill-advised efforts at masquerading but, conversely, she adamantly refused to let Mark guess how badly she was feeling about his discovery, or his pithy description of her and Guy's complicity, and with this in mind she dipped her head and remarked as nonchalantly as possible, 'If you say so, Mr Seymour,' as she brushed past him on the way to her room.

Minutes later she was in the shower, thankfully scrubbing away the accumulated dust and dirt of her wretched day, and inspecting the various bruises, cuts and burns she had somehow managed to acquire in the process. She was glad Mark had said her hands 'had been' like velvet, because they certainly couldn't be described that way now. At least two broken nails, a distinctly blotchy-looking burn and assorted pieces of missing skin definitely had not improved their appearance, she decided ruefully, as she looked over their roughened and deteriorated surfaces.

Back in her bedroom she dressed in a pair of dark red flared pants and a white polo-necked sweater, added a light covering of make-up and brushed some order into her curls before reluctantly returning to the kitchen where Chris was well into the preparation of the evening meal.

Warm blue eyes slid over her sympathetically. 'It does wonders, doesn't it? A hot shower after a day spent working outside?' Chris remarked in a friendly tone.

'Mmm, it—it certainly does,' Shannon agreed stiltedly, nervously fingering the fine linen cloth that would be used on the table that night, and feeling ill at ease because she had no idea just what Mark had told his sister and she wouldn't have liked Chris to believe only the worst about her.

For a moment neither of them spoke and then the older girl put out a tentative hand and suggested, 'Would you like to tell me about it?' A quick look at the wall clock and, 'We've got time—the kids are engrossed in the television— and the men won't be back for a while. Sometimes it helps to be able to talk things over with another person,' she smiled encouragingly.

Shannon eased on to one of the long-legged stools and rested her arms pensively on the smooth surface of the breakfast bar.

'Didn't *he* tell you?' she enquired bitterly.

Chris plumped down on to the next stool and shook her head cheerily. 'Not a word! Big brother can be very close-mouthed when he chooses to be. After muttering something completely incomprehensible under his breath—and I have the feeling it was just as well it wasn't said aloud—he stormed out of here almost as soon as you'd left and hasn't been seen since.'

'Probably gone to check whether the calves I branded this morning are still alive,' morosely.

'You couldn't have been that bad, could you?' Chris half laughed.

Shannon's eyes rose expressively upwards. 'Don't you believe it!' she adjured positively. 'Oh, Chris, I was hopeless!'

'In that case, perhaps you'd better start right at the beginning and tell me how you managed to convince Harry Crawford you'd been a jillaroo before and could do the work, eh?' she proposed gently.

Shannon nodded and sighed before launching into her story. It didn't take long to tell and by the time she had finished Chris was nodding her own head in understanding and a lively grin of enlightenment was playing over her features.

'I might have known Guy's name would crop up some-where along the line— he always was a madcap—but surely even he must have known you wouldn't be able to fool Mark into believing you were experienced. That young man deserves a good talking to!' she finished decisively.

'Oh, no!' Shannon came to her absent friend's defence immediately. 'It was as much my fault as his. I shouldn't have accepted the position when Mr Crawford offered it to me.'

'Maybe,' Chris assented thoughtfully, then, 'But what will you do now? Wait until a vacancy occurs for a first year jillaroo?'

'I suppose I shall have to. Your brother didn't exactly give me much choice once he found out.'

'No, darn him! Now I'm not at all sure just what I should do.'

'Why's that?'

'Because after meeting you yesterday I thought you were going to fit in extremely well and so I wrote to Paul—my husband—last night, telling him that I would definitely be leaving for home on Friday week ... and Don Ferguson took the letter with him to post in town for me this morn-ing.' A helpless shrug followed. 'Now, if I go ahead with my plans I shall be leaving Mark and Pete in a spot with no one to keep house for them, and if I don't leave then Paul's going to be terribly disappointed. He's been on at me for the last month or more asking when I'm going to return and I've only stayed as long as I have because it helped the men out since Beryl left to look after her ailing sister in Cootamundra.'

'I've certainly caused a lot of trouble, not only for myself but for everyone else as well, haven't I?' lamented Shannon.

Chris covered Shannon's hand with one of her own. 'You can't blame yourself for this,' she denied the younger girl's responsibility emphatically. 'You weren't to know I'd sent the letter off and I shouldn't have been quite so anxious to write to Paul until I was more sure of the facts, but that's me all over—too impulsive, I guess,' she grinned ruefully.

'Me too,' laughed Shannon in response. 'Otherwise I wouldn't be finding myself in this mess.' Then, more soberly, 'But what will you do, Chris? Will you stay, or leave?'

'Having written I think I shall have to leave, but in the meantime I shall pray like you know what that Harry can come up with a replacement. It's either that or persuade Mum to take over and,' she lowered her voice confidentially, 'just between the two of us, I'm not sure that Mark and Pete wouldn't prefer to manage on their own if that was the case. When Mum does consent to take a hand with the cooking you have to be prepared to have your meals when it fits in with her schedule, and that means you're likely to get your breakfast around the middle of the day, miss lunch altogether, and have a somewhat dried and burnt offering for dinner at ten o'clock in the evening,' she laughed reminiscently. 'Of course Betty Lovett would offer to help, but I don't think it's fair to ask her—she has enough to cook for already.'

Reflectively the two of them rose to their feet and moved back into the work area where Chris suddenly began rapping her knuckles thoughtfully on the top of the cupboard and turned to Shannon with a scheming look on her face.

'Unless, of course...' she murmured softly, almost to herself.

Intrigued, Shannon quickly queried, 'Unless ... what?'

'Would you be prepared to stay on here and do the housekeeping?'

Shannon blinked her surprise at the unexpected question and a light of hope began to sparkle in the depths of her blue eyes, but it was just as soon extinguished when she replied resignedly, 'Your brother would never agree to it. After what he had to say this afternoon he wouldn't accept me here now at any price.'

'Maybe—maybe not.' Chris moved her hands expressively. 'But would you stay if Mark did agree?'

Hunching her shoulders, Shannon thought the question over carefully. That would of course solve the problem of how she was going to get herself back to Sydney, and she had been determinedly pushing that particular worry to the back of her mind ever since Mark had fired her. The complication of the man himself she preferred not to even think about at all. Then there was the question as to whether she would be better off taking another job altogether—one which didn't only consist of housekeeping—but that immediately brought her back to her first difficulty. How was she going to get back to Sydney and find somewhere to live when she had no ready money? At least if she stayed on Tuesday for only a short while she wouldn't be quite so penniless when she left and maybe, just maybe, she could get Tony to teach her the rudiments of what a jillaroo was expected to know so she would be better prepared the next time she applied for a similar position. With her mind made up she nodded affirmatively to Chris, who was interestedly awaiting her reply.

'Yes, I'd stay,' she said, then bit at her lip uncertainly. 'Although I still can't see Mark approving the idea.'

'Yes, well, as you say, he might prove to be the stumbling block in our plans, but ...' she grinned incorrigibly, 'you haven't seen me in action yet, either!'

With a laugh Shannon exclaimed hurriedly, 'And I'd

better not, or he'll be sure to think it was my suggestion to take over in your place.'

'Mm.' Chris was already thinking ahead and tapped a fingernail consideringly against her teeth. 'I might even be able to rope Mum in on our side, because I know for certain she won't be keen when she finds out she'll be expected to do it otherwise.' She looked pleased with her thoughts. 'Hmm, all things considered, I believe we have a good chance of bringing brother Mark around to our way of thinking.'

'I hope so—for your sake, as well as mine,' was Shannon's sincere reply.

Shannon wasn't too sure what she had expected from Mark during dinner that evening—whether she had been prepared for him to regale them all with an account of her abysmal efforts during the day, or even to relate with a certain grim satisfaction the fact that he had found it necessary to dismiss her. But, whatever she had subconsciously been waiting for, it wasn't the total silence that he maintained throughout the meal regarding the subject and, in consequence, her gaze kept straying involuntarily in his direction, but apart from one slightly interrogating look in return for her not inconsiderable regard, he concentrated on the food before him in the main and made absolutely no mention of her at all.

For once Mrs Seymour took more than her usual vague interest in the general conversation as she described some of the sketches she had been working on and the ideas she wanted to put into practice the following day for completing the set which, as far as Shannon could gather, were to be placed on display at the Seymour Vale school's centenary celebrations which would be taking place early in the spring.

Immediately the meal was concluded Shannon swiftly

stacked the dishes in the automatic washer, made sure the kitchen was clean and tidy and then made her way to her room while Chris saw the children safely into bed for the night.

Closing the door behind her, she stood for a moment taking in the room's attractive decor and sighing disconsolately. She didn't really hold out much hope of Chris being able to change her strong-willed brother's mind regarding her dismissal, and laying one of her cases open on the bed she slowly began taking her clothes from the wardrobe, folding them neatly and placing them inside.

With most of her packing completed she paused to light a cigarette and opened the french doors so that she could stand by the verandah rail looking out over the dark tree-blackened landscape. The wind that had blown steadily all day had now eased, but in its place there was a crisp chill to the air which nipped maliciously at any areas of exposed skin and had her shivering and rubbing her hands up and down her arms in an effort to combat its insidious touch.

An unexpected sound behind her had Shannon spinning around to find Mark standing beside the open doors, arms loosely folded across his chest and lazily sure of himself as gold-flecked eyes roved unhurriedly over her creamy skinned features and he drawled, 'I see you're almost ready for your long hike back to the city.'

Taking a deep breath to steady her pulse after that close scrutiny, Shannon made herself smile back carelessly. 'That's right,' she endorsed his comment airily. 'It won't be long now and I'll be on my way,' endeavouring to make it sound as if the thought was decidedly appealing.

She knew she should never have considered Chris's idea —just the same as she shouldn't have gone along with Guy's. How doubly humiliating to be both fired from one positon and found unacceptable for another on the same day by the same person!

Mark eyed her narrowly from beneath dark brows. 'So

you had no intention of keeping your word to Chris,' he accused grimly.

'I'm not sure I know what you mean,' Shannon fenced, pressing her lips together unhappily.

'Sure you do, blue eyes!' His voice turning even colder now. 'So don't try any more of your misleading little stratagems on me! You know only too well what suggestion Chris just put to me.'

'Okay, okay! So I do know what you're talking about,' she admitted her knowledge defensively, pushing past him into the room and stubbing out her cigarette with shaking fingers before turning back belligerently. 'But as you saw,' she indicated the cases on the bed with an emotionally out-flung hand, 'I didn't need to wait for your answer, did I? I wouldn't presume to expect it to be anything else but a big fat *no*!' she flared.

With lithe grace Mark moved into the room and closed the glass-paned doors. 'You really are a little vixen when you're aroused, aren't you, Shannon?' he half smiled, leaning back against the doors casually and watching her, she thought, tauntingly.

His description swiftly brought to mind the events of the afternoon when he had used the word before, and Shannon found herself staring up at him wordlessly as she recalled the exciting pressure of his lips on her own and the sensuous feel of his hands against her skin. Swallowing hastily she dragged her eyes away from the rugged face before her and forced herself to retaliate as unconcernedly as was possible.

'And that's just one more reason to be rid of me, isn't it?' she queried with cool-sounding indifference. 'Think of the furore it would cause—and the insupportable example it would be for the rest of the staff if I should actually dare to answer the boss back!' with less coolness but more sarcasm.

To her wide-eyed astonishment Mark started to laugh, showing amazingly white teeth against the bronze of his skin, and sending nerve-tingling shivers down her spine.

'You think I couldn't find an effective way to curb your desire for repartee if I had to?' he provoked softly, a heart-stopping look in his eyes.

Ignoring the look and any implication it might contain, Shannon spun away and pretended interest in the odds and ends left on her bed which still had to be packed.

'Either way it's hardly relevant, is it?' she queried over one shoulder. 'I won't be here.'

'So I was right after all. No wonder you had that guilty look on your face again tonight.'

'I didn't have a guilty look on my face!' she expostulated indignantly, turning completely around this time.

'Didn't you?' sardonically.

'No!'

'Then why all the glances during dinner?'

'Because—because I ... oh, you know very well why!'

'Because you'd already decided to opt out,' he filled in for her. Shannon sank down wearily on to the side of the bed and shook her head despondently. 'Did I have much of an alternative?' she defended herself huskily. 'It was either that or have you do it for me.'

'Was it?'

A frown drew Shannon's arched brows closer together as she studied his enigmatic expression from the protection of long thick lashes. 'Well, wasn't it?'

Muscular shoulders rose and fell indolently. 'So you insist on telling me. Perhaps no one ever told you there's more than one answer that can be given to a question like that.'

'And they are...?' warily.

'Yes ... no ... or maybe,' came the bland reply.

Did that mean...? Or was he just trying to raise her hopes in order to deliver the final crushing blow? Shannon couldn't make up her mind and as a result her normally placid temper began to rise steadily.

'Why don't you just tell me what you came for and stop baiting me, Mark?' she demanded imperiously, although her words lost some of their effect when she realised she had inadvertently used his first name and added a rapid, 'Er—I mean, Mr Seymour,' as an amendment.

'Mark'll do,' he allowed lazily in response, hooking his thumbs into the wide leather belt encircling his waist. 'And the reason I came to see you was to find out for myself if what Chris told me was true. Are you willing to take on the housekeeper's position when she leaves, Shannon?'

'No jillarooing at all?' she whispered less than hopefully but making one last stand anyway.

His head moved uncompromisingly from side to side. 'Uh-uh! I think the stock received enough ministrations from you today to last them for many years to come. Definitely no jillarooing!' he decreed peremptorily.

Shannon accepted his conditions resignedly and murmured, 'Yes, I would like the housekeeper's position. That is, of course, if ...' she lifted one shoulder diffidently, 'you have no objections.'

His mouth curved devastatingly. 'None that I know of, blue eyes ... at the moment. Except to say I hope that so very slender figure of yours isn't a reflection upon your culinary ability.'

With her heart still racing uncontrollably from the effects of his smile, Shannon seized upon his remark like a drowning man to a straw, denying the chaos he was bringing to her emotions by seeking refuge in anger.

'I cooked for my father from the age of twelve and *he* seemed to like it!' she threw at him witheringly.

Mark paced leisurely to the door before taunting, 'Well, I can't say I care for your wording—"seemed" does somehow manage to leave a certain niggle of apprehension in one's mind—but no doubt the proof will be in the eating, as the saying goes,' and he had departed before she could frame another suitably sharp retort.

Even after Mark had been gone for some minutes his presence still seemed to invade the room illusively and Shannon irritably dragged another cigarette from the packet and allowed her indignation full rein in an attempt to dispel the disquieting impressions he caused upon her nervous system.

Inhaling briefly, she let her anger run on. How dared he comment upon her slightness! It was no business whatever of Mark Seymour's what her size was, and to suggest it might have been brought about as a result of her cooking was too infuriating to even think about. Once Chris left the property *then* let him make any disparaging remarks about her competence and he would really see how aroused she could become!

An anticipatory smile at the thought brought a challenging light to her intensely coloured eyes and an engaging sweep to the outline of her mobile mouth as she began slowly removing her clothes from the suitcases and replacing them in the wardrobe she had transferred them from such a short time before.

CHAPTER FIVE

'I TOLD you it would turn out okay, didn't I?' said Chris with a wink the following morning when the children had left the kitchen to get ready for school.

Shannon gave a wry grin. 'I bet you had to do some hard talking before Mark gave in to the suggestion, though,' she surmised ruefully.

'Not all that much,' Chris shook her head in emphasis, turning juicy steaks under the griller. 'In fact, I thought he seemed rather relieved at the idea of just not having to advertise again. It's so hard to get good station help these days.'

Searching in a drawer for the bread knife, Shannon began cutting thick slices from a crusty loaf, commenting over her shoulder, 'But what about the outside work? Wouldn't he have preferred someone who could do both?'

'Oh, it's not too bad while Pete's home and, at the moment, I think getting someone to look after the house was Mark's main concern. I suppose he figures he can always get another jillaroo later if he has to—when Pete leaves.'

Determinedly Shannon kept on with what she was doing. 'And does everyone know I was fired yesterday?' she speculated tentatively.

'I don't think so,' the older girl relieved her mind thoughtfully. 'Pete certainly never mentioned anything about it and I'm sure he would have done if he had known, and if he doesn't know then it's a safe bet that none of the others do either,' she smiled her encouragement.

Oh, well, that was some consolation at least, sighed Shannon. It was the first time she had ever been sacked from a job—or even been reprimanded over her work—and the chastisement still sat very heavily on her conscience, but it would have been almost intolerable if the rest of the staff had known as well.

'Winter's not far away,' predicted Tony with a graphic shiver a few minutes later when he brought the milk into the kitchen and proceeded to rub his hands together roughly to warm them. 'Half your luck, I expect you'll be back in the gulf country before it really arrives.' He gave Chris a mock envious grin.

'My word I will!' she agreed. 'I'll be off on Friday week and heading for warmer climes.'

'At least you'll be able to see the Show before you leave,' he said.

'Show? What Show's that?' Shannon broke in, looking from one to the other.

'Didn't you know?' returned Chris in surprise. 'The Narrawa Annual Show is on this Thursday, Friday and Saturday.'

A look of remembrance flickered over Shannon's face. 'That's right, I do remember now,' she said. 'I think Pete mentioned something about Mark getting his entrants ready for a Show the night before last.'

'Mmm, Mark always enters some of the stud stock. He's taken out the grand champion and junior champion bull awards for the last four years, and he had the senior female champion last year as well,' Chris recalled her brother's success proudly.

Shannon's mouth tilted obliquely. Of course, the auto- cratic Mark Seymour's stock wouldn't dare be anything but the best, but no sign of her antagonism was apparent when next she asked interestedly, 'And what else do they have at the Show besides cattle judging?'

It was Tony who related the different events with gusto. 'There's machinery displays, side shows, trotting races, all the usual equestrian events—including show-jumping— handcraft and produce exhibits, some rodeo events, and a good dance to finish it off on Saturday night,' he explained.

'In other words, it's good all-round entertainment, I gather,' laughed Shannon.

'Too right it is!' he applauded her opinion soundly. 'No one misses the annual shows. They're one of the big social events in the pastoral year.'

'That's true,' seconded Chris with a smile. 'You'll see just about the whole of the population from miles around converging on Narrawa at some time this week. The Show not only provides an opportunity to see what others have achieved in the industry in one form or another, but it's also a chance to renew acquaintances and catch up with all the information you've missed over the previous twelve months.'

'But didn't you go to your local show last year when you were in Queensland?' Tony suddenly enquired with a frown.

'Oh—er—no.' Shannon glanced wildly at Chris as if seeking help before giving a nervous laugh and stammering, 'I—er—arrived too late for one and—um—left a couple of weeks before the next.'

Accepting her explanation unsuspiciously, Tony headed for the door, then stopped and grinned.

'Never mind, you can still come and cheer for your co-employees this Saturday,' he suggested somewhat self-consciously.

'You mean you're competing in some of the events?' Shannon asked delightedly.

'Mmm,' he admitted laconically. 'In a burst of youthful enthusiasm last Saturday night in the hotel Don, Trevor, and myself convinced ourselves that it was our duty to up-hold the name of the station by taking part in the rodeo.'

'The buck-jumping?' laughed Shannon.

'Uh-huh ... and the bullock ride ... and the camp-drafting,' he related the events forlornly.

'Don't let him fool you, Shannon,' Chris interposed merrily. 'He's only after sympathy. The three of them can ride like they were glued to the saddle.'

'Thanks! Now she won't even bother to come and watch.' He gave Chris a darkening look of mock resentment which had both girls laughing.

'Oh, yes, I will. I wouldn't miss it for the world,' averred Shannon sincerely. 'I shall make sure I see every event you compete in. How's that?' she promised.

His satisfaction was made evident by a broad grin as he approved, 'Better and better. If I'd known that I might even have entered more of the contests,' almost wistfully.

'Breakfast not ready yet?' an injured voice proclaimed as

Pete pushed through the slightly open door, shrugging out of his thick jacket and tossing it, along with his hat, on to the settle. 'Come on, Chris, you know we have to get these cattle in to the showground today, and,' with a knowing grin in Tony's direction, 'you'd better not be too long either, because I saw Betty a moment ago and she was about ready to take the carving knife to you, son, for keeping her waiting. She's planning on going in the truck with Wade because she has an appointment for young Luke and Adrian to get their 'flu shots from the doctor this morning.'

'Oh, lord!' Tony's hand smote his forehead in dismay. 'She did mention it at dinner last night, but I clean forgot. I'll see you all later,' and with a resounding slam to the door he went out, and they could see him through the windows hurrying across the yard to his own quarters.

'Right,' Pete rubbed his hands together complacently. 'Get a move on, Chris, we've a lot to do this morning.'

'And we haven't, I suppose?' his sister pulled an indignant face at him. 'Don't worry, we won't hold you up, little brother. By the time you've washed, breakfast will be on the table.'

'I should think so too,' he teased in turn before disappearing into the hall.

'Huh!' Chris wrinkled her nose good-naturedly at the now empty doorway before returning to the griller and Shannon swiftly threw a gaily checked cloth over the table in the dining room and began laying out the necessary requisites for the meal. As she was putting the last touches to the small centre bowl of velvet-dark pansies, Mrs Seymour wandered thoughtfully into the room and gave her a kindly smile.

'That looks very nice, dear,' she complimented. 'I do so like to have flowers around me, they're such beautiful creations. Perhaps you would care to pick some more after breakfast and put them in my studio—if you have the time, of course,' she suggested quietly.

'I would be pleased to, Mrs Seymour,' Shannon answered warmly, glad to be able to do something for this very sweet-natured woman whose work she had admired for so long and, as soon as the meal was over and Chris had left to take the children to school, she happily set about arranging more of the soft purple, yellow and brown flowers in round vases and carefully carried them along to where Mrs Seymour's studio was located at the rear of the homestead, knocking lightly on the polished and panelled door.

Relieving her of one of the bowls, Mrs Seymour led the way into the spacious sunlit room where the skylight above them allowed nature's illumination to provide the necessary lighting for bringing to perfection Nola Seymour's artistry.

'Just put them wherever you can find a space, dear,' she suggested with a smile as she swept some half-completed sketches, pencils and brushes to one side of a small table facing the windows that took up most of the outside wall. 'Anywhere will do.'

Doing as she was bid, Shannon gently moved another assortment of papers into some semblance of a tidy pile on an amazingly cluttered desk and looked about her with interest.

'You like to look at paintings?' Mrs Seymour asked on seeing Shannon's preoccupation with the canvases that were spread about the room, some framed and mounted, others merely leaning in almost cavalier negligence against the pale walls.

'I wouldn't dare devalue them to the extent of calling them mere paintings,' Shannon returned with a self-effacing smile. 'I might not be a professional critic but, to my mind, that's *art*!' She waved a significant arm to indicate the collective works about the room. 'I don't think anyone manages to portray life in the Australian bush quite as well as you do.'

'How very sweet of you to say so,' Mrs Seymour seemed

genuinely pleased with the humble opinion, which Shannon found rather endearing when she knew quite well that the compositions had been lauded by some of the most discriminating judges in the land. 'Perhaps you would like to see some of the ones I've been working on recently?'

'Yes, please!' A pause. 'If it wouldn't be taking up too much of your time, that is,' unassumingly.

'No, no, it would be my pleasure,' Mrs Seymour smiled, and crossed to where a group of unframed canvases were propped against crowded bookshelves. 'These are some I've selected for my next exhibition in Sydney. You must tell me what you think of them.'

If the first was anything to go by Shannon knew exactly what she would think of them. It was marvellous! The subject and the colours so vibrantly alive! The picture was of a mounted stockman leaning slightly forward over his horse's slanting shoulders, reins held short and low, a whip coiled loosely in one hand; caught at that very second after heels had been put to his mount's sides and powerful hindquarters dipped for maximum thrust and long forelegs stretched out to accept the momentum of a rapid change in gait after a great bullock, its head proud, eyes wild, had broken from the mustered herd and begun its desperate, but doomed, dash for freedom.

The rider was dressed in undistinguished fawn drills, sleeves rolled up to show suntanned forearms, a hat pulled low on a dark head, but still Shannon knew his identity immediately. It was Mark. The authenticity was there in the unyielding set of his head, the width of shoulders, the muscular length of leg as it pressed to the horse's side, and the supreme male assurance that swirled about him like an invisible cloud.

The white-boled trees and the brilliantly blue sky were faintly but deliberately marred by the spiralling film of red dust rising from beneath the feet of the nervous cattle and

the finer detail receded into the distance, leaving all attention riveted to the central figure and incredibly capturing
the very essence of the man himself.

With a long-drawn-out sigh Shannon handed it back.
'It's beautiful,' she breathed softly, reverently almost, pay-
ing homage to her companion's ability to recreate so vividly
on canvas what had been viewed for one split second by the
human eye.

'You like it, then?' Mrs Seymour enquired with a
pleased look as she returned it to its resting place and chose
another for Shannon's inspection.

'Oh, yes, I think it's magnificent. It's—it's Mark, isn't
it?' Not that she really needed to ask.

'Yes, he makes such a good subject, don't you think?' A
hand indicated the painting Shannon had seen with her
father in Sydney and which hung peerlessly above the
mantel of the open fireplace. 'Even as a child he was good
material.' A tinkling laugh of remembrance. 'Reluctant,
mind you, but still very worthwhile.'

'I guess he must be used to it by now, then,' Shannon
smiled.

'I suppose so—at least, he never complains any more,'
Mrs Seymour confided candidly. 'Now what about this
one? Does that appeal to you?' And her second selection
was passed over for examination.

From then on Shannon was treated to a variety of paintings and sketches, which at times dazzled the eyes with
colour and movement, form and vigour, but which always
claimed attention imperiously whether it was a sketch of an
appealing little wagtail, an aggressive landscape of uniquely
natural bushland with a flock of pink and grey galahs
wheeling overhead, or an action-filled scene of stockmen,
torsos bare and bronzed, muscles flexed and rippling, as
they wrestled with fractious stock in the course of their
work.

It was more than an hour later before Shannon left the

studio. If there was one thing Nola Seymour wasn't vague about, it was art! On that subject she would, and could, converse quite happily for hours. So when Shannon finally emerged into the hall it was to find Chris coming towards her and exclaiming, 'So that's where you were! I wondered where you'd got to. Do you want to have your first lesson now? I've left the car out.'

Shannon's forehead creased. 'First lesson?' she queried.

'Didn't Mark say anything to you about it last night?' and on receiving a puzzled shake of the head for an answer, 'As you don't ride, he suggested I should teach you to drive before I left. Out here it's necessary that you should be able to do one or the other—and both for preference,' she explained. 'How about it?'

'I'm game, if you are,' Shannon laughed, pleased at the opportunity. She would have really liked to have attempted both, but was happy to settle for one at the moment. After Mark's flat refusal last night to allow her near any of the stock in future, learning to ride would probably have to be an ability she accomplished elsewhere. 'But do you think a week is long enough for me to learn?' she now asked.

'Well, I suppose that all depends on how quickly you pick it up, and how many lessons we can manage to fit in. Of course it's a lot easier out here because we don't have all that much traffic to worry about, and with the whole of the property to practise in it gives you a good chance to really get the feel of the car before you actually venture on to the road. Between the two of us I think we should be able to have you proficient enough to obtain your provisional licence before I leave,' Chris smiled.

For the rest of the morning Shannon slowly and cautiously manoeuvred the station wagon over the property, at times following the routes she had taken with Mark the day before, and at other times moving in entirely different directions. Not that she had much of a chance to observe any of the scenery, for she found she needed all her concentration to remember the instructions Chris had given her and to put them into practice at the right time, but gradually she discovered she was losing some of her tenseness and her actions were becoming a little more fluid with each tutored movement.

'That was great!' Chris applauded openly on their return to the homestead for lunch. 'A few more days like this and we'll have you reversing and doing three-point turns without blinking an eye,' she grinned. 'What did you think of it?'

Shannon wrinkled her nose self-consciously. 'I'm not sure,' she laughed. 'I think I was getting the hang of it, but please don't rush me into the rest of those things you mentioned. I'd hate to smash Mark's car, especially when that's exactly what his last jillaroo did,' with horror at the thought.

'No chance of that,' Chris discarded the idea off-handedly as they made their way across the verandah and into the kitchen. 'You did very well for your first time behind the wheel. Believe me, I know—because I was disgraceful when Dad first taught me,' she chuckled.

Perhaps so, mused Shannon ruefully, but she couldn't see that memory having any bearing on Mark's reaction should she inadvertently damage the vehicle during one of her lessons. He had made it all too clear what he thought about her performance with his livestock. If she started ruining his machinery as well she could imagine that really would bring the period of her employment on Tuesday to an abrupt and humbling end.

As the men were still engaged in settling the cattle at the showground there left only three women for lunch and, this quickly disposed of, Chris spent the afternoon showing Shannon over those parts of the large homestead she hadn't yet seen and explaining the routine running of the household. Apart from the house being so much more extensive than the flat she had shared with her father for the last nine years, Shannon didn't envisage any undue problems associated with its efficient management when the time came for Chris and the children to leave. In fact, she realised she was actually looking forward to putting Mark Seymour well and truly in his place by delving into her repertoire and bringing forth some of the more exotic dishes her father had enjoyed so much before his last illness.

Thursday was another quiet day on the property, as most of the men had gone into Narrawa to watch the cattle judging, and Chris availed herself of the opportunity to give Shannon another driving lesson, one which both of them were very pleased with, but which was somewhat overshadowed by their preoccupation with waiting to hear the results from the Show.

Dusk was readily approaching and turning the clouds overhead a hazy purple when the sound of dogs barking heralded the men's return. Chris and the children rushed out on to the verandah, peering through the half light excitedly, and Shannon, reluctantly, wasn't far behind them. She would have liked to have displayed a cool indifference to the proceedings altogether, but their enthusiasm was catching and she found she was waiting to hear whatever awards had been achieved almost as proprietorially as everyone else.

Pete was the first to bound up the steps on to the verandah, his hands clasped theatrically together above his head in a sign of victory.

'He's done it again!' he cried jubilantly, a broad grin splitting his cheerful face. 'Most successful exhibitor! Tuesday Park Overlord took out the Grand Champion ribbon; Tuesday Park Dominion won the Reserve Senior Championship; and Tuesday Park Heiress 10th was the Junior Champion Female.' He paused slightly for breath. 'And not only that, but we also won three firsts and two seconds in

the class judging. Along with their awards from the Sydney
and Brisbane Royals, it should make good advertising for
our next sale,' he crowed.

Still standing in the background in the encroaching dark-
ness, Shannon listened intently to Pete's information, her
breathing quickening unconsciously as she heard the
amount of blue ribbons the stud had won, and nearly
jumped out of her skin when a warm hand descended on to
her shoulder.

'Disappointed?' a low mocking voice whispered close
beside her, causing her lashes to flutter nervously as she
pulled restively away from the unsettling touch.

Surprisingly, she wasn't—but her amazement was also
tinged with some dismay that Mark should have guessed at
her original feelings so accurately. Could he really read her
antagonistic thoughts so clearly? If that was the case, she
would do well to develop a misleading defence and, to this
end, she pouted, unknowingly provocative.

'But of course I'm disappointed,' she agreed demurely.
'Couldn't you have managed to win the Grand Champion
Female ribbon as well?'

Mark's deep laughter had Chris swinging round immediately she realised her brother had joined the group.

'Mark! I didn't see you arrive. Congratulations! It's
nice to see some recognition for all those long hours you put
in throughout the year,' she exclaimed elatedly.

Now the children pushed into the gathering, clamouring
for their share of the attention. 'That was real beaut, wasn't
it, Uncle Mark?' Davey made his contribution in as grown-
up a tone as he was able, while Jane contented herself with
a shrill treble, 'Can we see the ribbons, Uncle Mark? Can
we see the ribbons?'

Smiling at the childish request, he rumpled Davey's hair
affectionately and swung his blonde-headed little niece high
in his arms to promise, 'On Saturday, when you come to
the Show. Okay?' before setting her down again after her

happy acquiescence, and Chris's prompting, 'You'd better tell Mum the good news. I don't expect she realises you're back yet,' had them all trooping into the welcoming warmth of the homestead.

For once Mrs Seymour joined their company in the lounge room after dinner that night and, of course, the talk centred around the day's events at the Show and, more particularly, all aspects of the cattle judging. However, this time it was Mark who excused himself from the gathering early in the evening, saying he had work he wanted to finish for the school's Centenary Committee. No sooner had he left the room than Chris shook her head in exasperation.

'You would think, tonight of all nights, Mark could afford to leave that office work for once, wouldn't you?' she questioned everyone in general. 'What he needs is a wife! That would certainly take his mind off business matters for a while,' she chuckled at her own suggestion.

'Could do, could do,' agreed Pete with an answering grin. 'And I hear Hilary Donovan's back home again.'

Instant interest implanted itself on Chris's face. 'Who told you that?' she wanted to know.

'Brian Hopwood, and he should know—he lives next door.'

'Well, isn't that interesting?' mused Chris with no little gratification. 'Mark and Hilary, eh? They always were close, even as kids.'

'And she's such a nice girl too.' Nola Seymour surprisingly had something to say on a matter which was far removed from that with which she normally occupied herself—but maybe she considered this was an exceptional circumstance.

Inexplicably the mention of the unknown and unseen girl's merits had a depressing effect upon Shannon, one which she steadfastly refused to analyse—and in an effort to dispel the dejecting thoughts she rose swiftly to her feet and muttered she would make more coffee, fleeing the room before Chris could make an offer to help. She preferred to settle her disquieting thoughts on her own.

A short time later she was back, her feelings strictly under control once more, with a heavily laden tray and another pot of steaming coffee. When everyone had what they required she turned to Chris hesitantly.

'I brought an extra cup and saucer, just in case. Do you think Mark would like another cup too?' she asked.

'Probably,' Chris replied with a nod. 'I usually take him one during the evenings when he's working.'

It didn't take long to ascertain that Mark liked his coffee black with very little sugar and having poured it to Chris's instructions, Shannon left the room and started down the hallway. The door to the office was slightly ajar and through the opening she could just see him impatiently turning over the papers on his desk, obviously searching for something he had misplaced. Tentatively she put a hand to the door, but before she could actually take a step forward Mark's voice reached out to her a trifle irritably.

'For heaven's sake, Shannon, either come in, or move on—but don't stand there dithering faint-heartedly!'

The unexpectedness of his remark had Shannon gasping, but not for long, for now she thrust open the door determinedly and marched up to the desk with a challenging look.

'I'm neither faint-hearted nor a ditherer, Mark Seymour!' she flared resentfully, placing the cup and saucer on his desk none too carefully. 'Stupid, perhaps, for even considering you might like another coffee and not wanting to disturb you unnecessarily, but then what could you expect from—from a deceitful little cat like me?' she questioned sarcastically. 'Or did you think I was spying on you in order to sabotage your office routine in some way?' facetiously.

Mark leant back lazily in his chair, arms folded across

his chest. 'Why limit yourself to the office?' he asked with a sardonic lift to one eyebrow. 'From your attempts last Tuesday I was beginning to wonder if you weren't endeavouring to sabotage the whole damned property!' which brought a rosy flush of embarrassed recollection to Shannon's cheeks. 'As to the other,' he continued in the same drawling tone, 'what I *think* is that you're going to need an extremely tight rein kept on you, blue eyes, otherwise that impulsive tongue of yours will tempt retribution once too often.'

With his previous form of punishment still foremost in her mind, it took Shannon a few seconds before she could rally her defences to retort as scornfully as possible, 'A typical chauvinist's attitude! Whatever we do, we mustn't provoke the male of the species, must we?'

'Not if you know what's good for you,' he agreed aggravatingly. 'And don't try sharpening those feline claws of yours on me, Shannon, because you just might find that my ideas of retaliation don't coincide with yours,' he cautioned enigmatically.

'You mean I might get slapped next time instead?' she just had to ask, brows winging insolently.

Casually Mark moved forward on his chair, lit a cigarette and eyed her narrowly through the blue-grey smoke that was curling upwards between them.

'There is another possibility you appear to have overlooked,' he advised ironically, resting his elbows on the desk and clasping one hand about the other in front of him.

'And that is?' prompted Shannon from beneath thick lashes.

His mouth tilted subtly at the look of uncertainty hovering deep within her eyes and he deliberately took his time before taunting softly, 'I'm not averse to firing you twice, blue eyes. I've done it once and I can just as easily do it again if I have to, although I can assure you there will be no reprieve the second time around. If I'm forced to dismiss you again... then you'll stay dismissed, little cat! Understand?'

Shannon drew a deep steadying breath at this inflexible ultimatum, not for one moment doubting that Mark wouldn't be as good as his word, but at the same time it was impossible for her to keep all of the rebellion from showing on her face as she retorted, 'Yes, boss!' with goading accentuation.

'And you can cut the sarcasm!'

Could she? That was what he thought, decided Shannon mutinously. 'Oh, but I wasn't...' she gave him a sweet look of innocence. 'I mean, that *is* how Chris introduced you, and that *is* what the men call you—isn't it? I just thought it would be appropriate if I did the same, that's all,' she murmured ingenuously, hands spread wide to emphasise her sincerity.

'Did you?' His amber eyes interrogated her levelly until she found herself flushing involuntarily under his perceptive regard and dropping her gaze to the vicinity of the desk top, whereupon he immediately questioned, 'I wonder why?' in a singularly dry tone.

'Well, I wouldn't want anyone thinking I was getting preferential treatment,' she offered in assumed self-effacing humility.

'Don't worry ... you won't!' came the swift unequivocal reprisal. 'I've no intention of allowing you to disrupt the smooth running of this property any more than you have done already, believe me!'

At last Shannon raised her eyes to his, but they were glowing with resentment when they did so. 'Oh, yes, you just have to keep bringing that up, don't you?' she flashed at him bitterly. 'Make one mistake on Tuesday and you're never allowed to forget it! Perhaps, to return the favour, I should keep reminding you of your barbarous behaviour that afternoon too!' she cried scornfully.

'I shouldn't if I were you,' Mark warned with such a lazy half smile that Shannon's pulse began beating crazily at the base of her throat and she bit at her lip in confusion when he stubbed out his cigarette and rose lithely to his feet to rest his hands on slim hips and goad, 'Or it might bring to mind the memory that it at least had the effect of silencing you, blue eyes.'

The mere thought of her response on that occasion was enough to have her taking hasty backward steps, suddenly eager to place more distance between them, and gulping nervously before attempting to return to an attacking position.

'The—the name's Shannon ... not "blue eyes" ... or "little cat"!' she blustered. 'And—and you might find the outcome quite different next time,' she tried to counsel repressively, only to utter a small, 'Oh,' of embarrassment on seeing one of his brows slanting upwards suggestively as she realised that her words had been tantamount to an open invitation, and promptly stammered, 'Not—not that there will be a next time, mind you,' in a throaty rejection of his glance.

'And that could just depend on how well you manage to control that lively tongue of yours, couldn't it?' he proposed idly.

'Could it?' she counter-questioned just as sardonically in an effort to regain her own emotional equanimity which seemed to have been unbalanced ever since she had first met this man. 'Well, with a threat like that hanging over my head you'll certainly have no worries in the future regarding my conduct, will you? I mean to say, "once bitten, twice shy" would seem to me to be an extremely appropriate line of thought to follow in these circumstances ... wouldn't you agree?' She turned demure blue eyes upwards.

'Quite so,' he averred with a sharp nod and an annoying disregard for her intended snub. 'And especially if you always return a man's kisses so provocatively. That un-inhibited response of yours could land you in trouble one of these days, blue eyes,' he cautioned coolly, passing her to pick up a folder from the filing cabinet before returning to his seat.

Never had Shannon felt quite so humiliated. That he should think her response of that fateful afternoon had been normal brought a crimson tide of heat to her cheeks that she couldn't control, and had her biting at her lip in dismay as she focused on his downbent head irresolutely. What could she say in her own defence? That her reactions weren't usually so shameless, but it just happened to be the effect he had on her? She shook her head mutely. She was sure he wouldn't believe her, but even if he did, that would only make her impetuosity seem all the more ignominious. She sighed dismally and turned for the door.

'Oh, by the way, Shannon,' Mark called after her. 'That's yours,' he indicated with his pen a neatly tied brown paper parcel resting on top of a cupboard by the door when she looked back at him apprehensively.

'Mine? What is it?' She frowned perplexedly at him, but he had gone back to his writing.

'I've no doubt you'll find out ... if you open it,' he recommended without lifting his head.

Slowly—suspiciously almost—Shannon approached the parcel and began fumbling with the string. It was a while before she had managed to undo the knots and pull away the paper to reveal the contents, but when she did so she gave an almost audible gasp of admiration. A sheepskin jacket! Something she had never been able to afford to buy for herself—with her father's illness lasting for so long there had always been other things she had needed to spend her money on—and one hand smoothed almost devoutly over the unbelievably soft fleece. Abruptly she snatched her hand away and deliberately turned her back on it.

'You know I haven't got the money for one of those,' she accused reproachfully.

His eyes met hers slowly. 'Did anyone suggest you should have?'

'But it will take me months to pay you back!'

'I haven't asked you to do that either,' he pointed out with resigned patience.

'No, you haven't,' she was forced to agree. 'But I don't make a habit of accepting gifts like that from men either!' she told him in no uncertain terms.

'You will in this instance, though!' inexorably.

'I will not! There—there might be all sorts of strings attached,' she couldn't help gibing.

Mark's eyes narrowed and Shannon could see the muscles in his jaw stiffen. 'Put your mind at rest, blue eyes! The coat was purchased with employer protection in mind, rather than employee seduction!' he cut her down to size mercilessly. 'As you are probably intending to visit the Show during the next couple of days, where I might add, the wind can slice across the grounds like a knife, then I took the opportunity of protecting my own interests by purchasing that jacket. With Chris leaving next week I can't afford to have my provisional housekeeper down with pneumonia when I'm trying to prepare for the school's centenary and the stud's next sales,' in coldly crushing tones.

Not that it was any consolation, but Shannon ruefully surmised she had recklessly invited that utterly deflating detraction, and she hadn't missed his 'provisional housekeeper' either! Obviously he was still in some doubts as to her suitability for the position, so, with her head angled disdainfully—she wasn't about to let him know how abrasive his words had been—she picked up the jacket, slung it nonchalantly over one shoulder and shrugged.

'Well, in that case, it might take a while, of course ...

but I will repay you,' she announced as insouciantly as she could in the face of the darkening look that was making its way across Mark's features. 'How much a week do you think would be a fair reimbursement?'

'I said there was no need!'

'I'm sorry, but I don't happen to agree with you. I mean to say, I...'

'Shannon!' His voice carried a soft but indisputable warning as it encompassed her. 'If you intend to still be working on this property in the morning, you'll get out of here ... right now! Or, so help me, I'll...'

She went—without even waiting to hear what Mark contemplated. She considered she had reached the stage where discretion demanded her withdrawal if she was to escape with any of her dignity intact at all.

CHAPTER SIX

As it happened, Shannon was very thankful to be able to shrug the warmth of a sheepskin jacket about her gold and tan-clad figure when she had finished dressing on Saturday morning. Although the sun was shining and the wind wasn't too noticeable, the temperature had dropped considerably during the preceding twenty-four hours and she was glad of the extra protection it would afford from the wintry elements outside.

In the kitchen Mrs Seymour was talking to Davey while Chris made some last-minute adjustments to Jane's woollen tam-o'-shanter and Mark and Pete, dressed similarly to Shannon with regard to their coats, leant against the verandah rail outside, talking earnestly.

On seeing her enter the room Pete immediately broke off his conversation with Mark to call, 'Come on out here, Shannon, we'll be leaving fairly soon,' and when she had moved up beside them he smiled, 'I see you're all wrapped up against the weather. Best things for keeping out the cold, eh?' fingering the soft lining of her lapel.

Before replying her gaze flicked impulsively to Mark, but he was apparently absorbed in his sweeping contemplation of the horizon, for no comment was forthcoming, and she shyly offered, 'I think so,' in reply.

The next minute the two children came hurrying out on to the verandah and proceeded to clamber over the back seat with all the exuberance of the very young into the rear of the station wagon parked beside the steps. For the drive into town Shannon discreetly manoeuvred herself into the back seat between Chris and her mother, leaving the front free for the men. The miles were soon slipping quickly by and while she could faintly hear what Chris was saying in the background, Shannon fell into a reverie of her own and tried to dissect her contrary emotions while, from time to time, surreptitiously eyeing Mark by way of the rear vision mirror.

That he had a vitally masculine attraction she would readily admit, although she wasn't so eager to confess, even to herself, that it was an irrevocable one where she was concerned. After all, an answer still had to be found for the illogical antipathy she could feel exploding inside her whenever they came into contact. Just because he had caught her unawares and extracted an overwhelming response from her with one kiss, there was no reason to suppose the result would be the same if it ever happened again.

No, she decided assertively, it had only happened that way because of the circumstances surrounding her employment, and the sooner she came to realise that fact the sooner she would be able to treat Mark Seymour as she had every other of her employers! But she found the decision easier to

make than the resolution to keep, for when she eventually
came out of her musings it was to find Mark patiently holding the car door open for her and, with what had recently
become characteristic perverseness, she pretended she
hadn't seen him and scrambled out of the vehicle behind his
stepmother on the opposite side.

On entering the showgrounds Shannon looked about her
with interest. Of course she had been to the Sydney Royal
Show—what child in that city hadn't, one Easter or another?—and here she was seeing exactly the same thing,
only on a smaller scale. There were the same expectant
crowds in holiday mood; the exhibits filled with agricultural machinery of all types and designs; sideshow opera-
tors displaying gaudily adorned prizes; travelling canteens
advertising their stock-in-trade with microphones—perhaps
not as harmoniously as in days long gone, but just as
effectively all the same; and over all could be heard the
muted commentary coming from the loudspeakers around
the showring, together with the champing and stamping of
penned animals.

Almost immediately they had passed through the gates
Mark and Pete had been claimed by a small group of men,
their dress singling them out as prosperous graziers, and
they now appeared to be deep in conversation while the
children began pleading with their mother to be taken to
the animal nursery.

'Okay, okay,' Chris finally agreed to their requests with a
smile, then, 'What about you, Mum ... Shannon? Are you
coming too?'

Shannon checked quickly with her wristwatch before
shaking her head regretfully. 'Much as I'd like to, I think
I'd better save it for later, thanks, Chris. Tony said the first
rounds of the campdrafting would be held early this morning and as I promised I'd watch, I think I had better be
heading for the ring.'

'I'll go with you too, dear,' Mrs Seymour proposed

quietly to Shannon. 'The days when I found enjoyment in traipsing around the stalls are far behind me, I'm afraid. For the last few years I've preferred to spend my time in the stands,' she said.

'Well, we'll see you later, then,' smiled Chris, beginning to move after the children who were already well on their way to the nursery. 'I expect I'll catch up with you some time, somewhere, before lunch,' with a laugh.

Leaving the men with their companions, Mrs Seymour set off at a brisk pace towards the ring and after showing her member's ticket at the gate, and receiving a complimentary one for Shannon, they made their way high into the covered pavilion where, at that time of the morning, they still had quite a large range of seats to choose from and could gain an uninterrupted view of the whole of the grass-covered arena.

In the sunshine below them a squad of men had nearly finished setting out the course and the small, slender saplings which represented the pegs and gates were rustling gently in the breeze which swirled unimpeded across the grounds. Now the grandstands began filling with more spectators, many of whom called greetings to Nola Seymour and included Shannon in their friendly waves. Around the outside of the ring most of the seats were taken and a large crowd had begun to assemble about the cutting out yard beside the rough riders' chutes. From her high vantage point Shannon could already see the mob of some ten or twelve steers in the yard and the first of the competitors, mounted and ready to go, as he waited by the judges' enclosure.

While the commentator announced his name over the loudspeakers, as well as that of his horse, the first entrant trotted through the gates into the small yard and the camp-draft was under way. Fascinated, Shannon watched while the rider swiftly looked over the herd pressing their way agitatedly around the pen, then, having made his choice, interposed his mount between the steer and the rest of his fellows, and by wheeling and turning, first in one direction and then another, thwarted the Hereford's natural instinct to return to the rest of his kind.

The man appeared cool and efficient in his handling of his mount, while the horse itself seemed delighted to be able to change legs and pace faster than their captive to ensure the steer never received a chance to outmanoeuvre him, and once he had been completely separated from the small herd the gate into the ring was opened and the horse sprang into a gallop in order to head the beast off before he could put too much distance between them.

Now the skill of the stockhorse and his rider really became visible. Thinking almost as one, they drove the steer around the first peg, then galloped up on its offside flank to wheel it around the second, and immediately dropped back to cross behind the animal and move up to its nearside shoulder, leaning into it in order to make it curve back around the same obstacle but in the opposite direction this time, then it was back around the first peg once more to finish their execution of a figure eight, down through the sapling gate and the round was over before the bell signalling the end of their forty-five seconds for the course had rung. It had been a thrilling display of co-ordination between horse and rider and as Shannon put her hands together with the rest of the crowd she speculated that it was going to be difficult for anyone to better the exhibition of that first competitor.

The next contestant experienced bad luck in that his steer slipped badly around the first peg and, in so doing, completely unbalanced the horse racing alongside him, with the result that both horse and rider came down heavily in a tangle of thrashing legs. Fortunately, however, the stockman was thrown clear and both managed to regain their feet without appearing to have suffered any undue damage. But, of course, there was no chance for them to complete their round within the allotted time and despondently they left the ring together.

And so the morning wore on. Shannon was glad to see that Tony managed to finish his rounds without any mishaps, but Don lost control of his steer after having traversed three-parts of the course, and Trevor's went charging to the opposite side of the ring before he had a chance to overtake it and, thereafter, attempted to turn the contest into a personal duel by continually hooking his horns towards the underside of Trevor's mount.

Mrs Seymour helpfully supplied Shannon with some of the finer points relating to the campdraft, but mostly she was absorbed with the sketchbook and pencils she had brought with her; recreating with sure, skilful strokes the various groups of people present, the contestants, and the atmosphere of the Show as a whole. When the last of the entrants had completed their courses and the judges' decisions were made public, Shannon smiled happily to hear that Tony had been awarded third prize and it wasn't long afterwards that she espied him outside the pavilion, beckoning for her to join him.

'No, my dear, that's quite all right. You run along and enjoy yourself,' replied Mrs Seymour to the query if she would mind if Shannon left to see more of the exhibits. 'I prefer sitting here, and the show-jumping's next. I always watch that,' she told the younger girl with a smile.

Tony linked his arm with Shannon's once she had come through the gate, and pushing his hat to the back of his head began leading her away from the grandstand.

'Congratulations! Did I bring you luck?' she smiled up at him teasingly.

'Must have,' he acknowledged with a grin. 'I've never done that well before.' He brought them both to a standstill and looked down at her enquiringly. 'Now, where would you like to go?'

'I'm easy,' she shrugged equably. 'Although I would like

to see the animal nursery some time today, if that's okay with you?'

'Sure, it's as good a place as any to start.'

'We might even run across Chris and the children. That's where they were heading the last time I saw them.'

'Could do,' Tony conceded as they began walking again. 'But I doubt it. Those two imps will have dragged Chris halfway around the showground by now, unless I miss my guess.'

The nursery was a delight to Shannon, watching the kiddies as they exclaimed, fondled and played with lambs, calves, foals, kids, chicks, ducklings, kittens, puppies and even a couple of piglets—nicely cleaned and spruced up for the occasion. But even as Tony had predicted, Jane and Davey were nowhere in sight and they continued with their sightseeing without catching a glimpse of Chris or any of the other members of her family.

It was going on for lunchtime before Shannon had finished admiring the livestock—and especially the award winners from Tuesday Park Stud; gazing awestruck at the size of some of the machinery on display; exclaiming over the handcrafts entered for judging; and browsing slowly through the small manufacturers' pavilion where all sorts of small goods and products were being demonstrated.

Approaching sideshow alley Tony's steps began to slow. He reached a hand upwards to brush the back of his wrist across his forehead and settled his hat more securely upon his head.

'I don't suppose you'd care to come to the dance with me this evening, would you, Shannon?' he finally asked in a rather diffident voice.

Surprised at his nervousness in asking her, Shannon gave him a sparkling smile. 'I'd love to, Tony,' she accepted his invitation readily. 'What time does it start?'

'Well, they have a dinner first—which the boss and his

family usually attend—along with most of the other property owners in the distrtict,' he relayed cheerfully, his uncertainty now a thing of the past. 'But the dancing begins around nine and goes till the early hours of the morning. I think you'll enjoy yourself.'

'I'm sure I shall. Thank you for asking me.'

'That's okay,' he laughed a little self-consciously. 'I was only surprised someone else hadn't beaten me to it.'

A few minutes later and they had come across the crowd surrounding the dunking pool where a man in his early forties, dressed in what earlier that morning must have been a beautifully tailored lounge suit, but which was now shapelessly bedraggled and waterlogged, was sitting on a plank suspended above the water while members of the crowd threw balls at the target above him in order to release the mechanism which would drop him once more into the pool below.

'Heavens, he's keen!' Shannon grinned, although she couldn't quite keep an imaginative shudder from appearing. 'Although I would have thought he'd wear something a little more appropriate than a suit.'

'Oh, no, that's half the fun,' Tony decried the suggestion immediately. 'The money all goes to charity and everyone who takes a turn on the plank is a volunteer. That's Les Walters up there now—he's the local bank manager,' nodding towards the hapless man who, just at that moment, took another sudden plunge amid good-natured cheering from the spectators. 'Want to take a turn?' Tony now asked with a twinkle.

'No, thanks!' Shannon vetoed the idea with a laugh, knowing he was only joking even though he caught hold of her hand lightly and began pulling her deeper into the crowd, calling over their heads to the operator, 'Hey, Charlie! I think we've found another one for you.'

Suddenly a heavy arm dropped on to Shannon's shoul-

ders, effectively breaking the grasp Tony had on her fingers
and halting their progress while a deep voice counter-
manded, 'I think not!' peremptorily.

Shannon found Mark's presence too close for comfort
and the weight of his arm about her shoulders infinitely
disturbing and made a fractious movement to pull away,
but his fingers tightened tenaciously and she was left no
option but to stay tormentingly close to his lean hard length
as he told Tony smoothly, 'I've sent Don down to the cattle
pavilion to relieve Wade. I think you'd better do the same
for Gordon for a couple of hours.'

'Right, boss,' Tony accepted the duty evenly, then, with
a wink at Shannon, 'I'll see you later,' and he was moving
out of the crowd with a purposeful step.

Only now did Mark look down at Shannon and she was
astonished to see such unbridled anger on his face as he
demanded, 'Haven't you any more brains than to let yourself be talked into something like that?'

Stung by what she considered to be the unfairness of his
reprimand, Shannon swung rebellious eyes upward and
retorted swiftly, 'He was only joking! And,' she waved an
arm in the direction of the pool, 'it is for charity, after all.
Your bank manager doesn't seem to mind!'

'Why should he? It was all arranged beforehand and he
came prepared—as did most of those who will be partici-
pating today,' he pushed his words home satirically. 'It's
usually only the older teenagers out for a good time and, as
often as not, with one or two beers too many under their
belts, who drag themselves up there out of the blue to make
a spectacle of themselves for their friends!'

'I was not planning to make a spectacle of myself!' she
snapped angrily, annoyed at the subtle innuendo that she
would have enjoyed making an exhibition of herself. 'As
I've already told you, Tony was only joking when he suggested I volunteer.'

'Sometimes jokes backfire! Or haven't you ever found

yourself in a position where you end up agreeing to some idea you had absolutely no intention of acceding to?'

'Well, yes, I have,' she had to admit slowly, but her voice tightened almost immediately to add sarcastically, 'But I'm surprised you should know of the feeling. I can't imagine anyone making you agree to something you didn't want to do!'

'Which just goes to show how wrong you can be. I re-hired *you*, didn't I?'

As the sardonic and hurtful words flowed over her, Shannon could feel the stain of humiliation rushing over her cheeks and she lowered her head so that Mark couldn't see just how much pain his deflating remark had caused, and when he began shepherding her along the alleyways between the sideshows she kept pace beside him silently, hoping against hope her inner turmoil wasn't visible.

Why his words should have upset her so much she really couldn't have explained with any amount of certainty. She had known all along that Mark would have preferred to see her leave his property and it had only been due to Chris's impulsive action in writing to her husband so expeditiously, thus leaving them in the lurch with regard to a housekeeper, that he had reconsidered his actions in firing her. Too often, and in too many ways, he had made it patently clear that he regarded her as a burden to be borne stoically only until such time as the position could be remedied to his satisfaction. So why had his words hurt so much? He was only confirming what she already knew, and although the knowledge wasn't very pleasant it still shouldn't have the power to stab so deeply, nor quite so intensely.

An amused sounding, 'Lost your tongue, little cat?' brought her out of her daydream abruptly, but she refused to raise her gaze to his, knowing full well that when he spoke in that particular tone there was always an accompanying look in his tawny eyes that tumbled her emotions into capricious disorder and had her heartbeat increasing tempestuously. Instead she muttered a defensively tart, 'No! Just guarding it,' and kept walking.

'Very wise—I'm glad to see you're finally learning.'

Shannon came to a decided halt, at last managing to spin out of the circle of that disturbing arm to face him, and now her blue eyes slanted furiously, her protective attitude quickly forgotten.

'Oh, yes, that's right, isn't it? I keep forgetting!' she responded sarcastically. 'If I want to keep my job then I'm expected to defer to the old tradition which advocates that women, like good children, should be seen but not heard and, even then, preferably only in the kitchen and bedroom!'

'It's an evocative theory,' Mark conceded with that amused glint in his eyes which could produce such disastrous effects upon her equilibrium. 'Although not quite what I had in mind. However, if you . . .'

Whatever he had been about to say was lost, for just then a light voice could be heard calling behind him, 'Mark! Mark! Wait for me!' and they both turned expectantly to watch the newcomer's approach.

Critically Shannon ran her eyes over the other girl, guessing her age to be a few years short of Mark's, and taking in the olive green flared slacks showing beneath a fur-trimmed chocolate suede jacket and the bright green and yellow scarf knotted about her throat. Small but slender, with long waving, light brown hair and hazel eyes, she hurried up to them with a wide smile curving her lips and placed a familiar hand on Mark's arm.

'It's good to be home again,' she sparkled up at him warmly. 'How have you been?'

Mark tilted his head consideringly and his glance brushed over Shannon's still slightly mutinous features momentarily before he replied with a wry twist to his well-shaped mouth, 'Not too bad, thanks, little one . . . all things considered. And you?'

'Just great ... *now*,' she laughed back at him, and they both smiled before Mark turned to say, 'Shannon, I'd like you to meet a neighbour of ours—Hilary Donovan,' and to the girl whose hand still rested on his arm, 'Shannon Marshall, our ...'

'You don't have to tell me—I already know. You should know how fast news travels up here, Mark,' Hilary interrupted with a smile, and held out her hand to Shannon, saying, 'So you're Tuesday's jillaroo. I'm very pleased to meet you, Shannon—I hope you'll enjoy your time on the tablelands.'

Shannon murmured a quiet, 'Thank you,' and briefly clasped the small warm hand extended towards her. So this was the girl that the family had been discussing the other night, and coupling her name with Mark's. From the emphasis Hilary had placed on her words and the term Mark had used, it was obvious to Shannon that these two were more to each other than mere neighbours and, inexplicably, she felt her heart go heavy at the thought and the breeze that had been growing stronger during the morning now seemed far more biting than it had a few moments ago, making her shiver and thrust her hands deeper into the pockets of her coat.

With a brave attempt at an indifferent smile to encompass the two beside her, she shrugged lightly and proposed, 'I'm sure you two must have a lot to talk about and I think I had better see if I can locate Chris and the children before lunch. It's nice to have met you, Hilary,' as she began to move away.

'Hey there! Not so fast!' A firm hand gripped her arm and brought her to a stop after only two steps had been taken. 'Chris and the rest of the family are already in the lunch rooms. That's where we were headed when Hilary stopped us.'

Without relinquishing his hold, Mark held out an inviting hand to the other girl. 'What about you, Hilary?' he enquired. 'Why don't you join us for lunch too?—you're very welcome.'

Shannon didn't doubt *that* for one moment and irritably wrenched her arm from Mark's fingers to stand cheerlessly watching as Hilary gave a rueful pout and lamented, 'Much as I'd love to, I'm afraid I can't, Mark. Dad has a prospective buyer with him and I promised I would have lunch with them.' A sudden thought brought a happy smile to her face. 'But I will see you tonight, won't I? I'll reserve every dance for you,' she twinkled engagingly.

'And I'll keep you to that,' Mark laughed before Hilary began hurrying back the way she had come, and Shannon's nails dug viciously into the palms of her hands in an effort to remind herself that his devastating smile had been meant for Hilary alone, and that she was a fool to allow herself to become so affected by one man's inherent masculinity.

'Which reminds me...' Mark began obscurely as they continued on their way to the lunch rooms, causing Shannon to glance obliquely at him from the corner of her eye with a frown. 'The dinner-dance tonight,' he enlightened her casually. 'You will be attending along with the rest of the family, of course.'

No sign of an invitation or a request, Shannon noted mutinously. Just a plain overbearing statement of irrefutable sureness! Well, she had news for Mark Seymour. She had already made other arrangements, and promptly proceeded to take great delight in haughtily informing him of that fact.

'Then you'll just have to cancel them, won't you?' came the imperturbable response.

At the blatant disregard for her plans, Shannon gasped and retaliated stormily, 'I will not! I can please myself whom I spent my time with when I'm not working!'

'Which statement, once again, proves how wrong you are.'

'And just what's that supposed to mean?'

Mark stopped walking and held her angry gaze with a relentless one of his own. 'It means, my blue-eyed little cat, that you'll do as you're told, or you'll find yourself dumped —bag and baggage—outside the gates of my property!'

Tears of frustration pricked at the back of Shannon's eyes and she blinked hurriedly before retorting, 'Is that how you control all your staff? By threatening them with the sack whenever one of them disagrees with you?'

'No, only the ones who try passing themselves off as something they're not! You should have had Guy explain a little more fully just what being a jillaroo entails,' he mocked annoyingly. 'It's no small responsibility for station owners to find themselves accountable for young, single girls who've decided they would like to work on the land. But in return for being treated as one of the family, as most of them are, they tacitly agree to accept the same type of parental control they would receive at home!'

'Well, I'm sorry, but I definitely don't think of you as a substitute father, Mark Seymour!' she found the courage to defy him. 'And I certainly never had to suffer your type of standover tactics from either of my parents anyway!'

'Perhaps it would have been better if you had,' he taunted coolly. 'Then you might not have found yourself agreeing to your boy-friend's bird-witted scheme that brought you here in the first place, and which is the cause of your now being placed in what you obviously consider to be a very unwelcome position.'

Unwelcome was right—although Shannon felt that un-endurable might have been a more accurate description! However, she still had an ace of her own to play and she gave him a facetious look from beneath long lashes.

'But I'm not a jillaroo any more, am I?' she reminded him sweetly. 'I'm a housekeeper now, s-o-o ...' drawing the word out pointedly, 'those rules don't apply in my case.'

Unfortunately her period of triumph was short-lived, for Mark merely treated her to a disparaging look, and catching hold of her arm once more started propelling her along beside him, informing her curtly, 'The rules apply when I say so, Shannon. All you have to do is make sure you abide by them.'

'Gee, *thanks*, you're all heart!' she declared in mock-appreciation, the darkening colour of her black-lashed eyes giving her creamy-skinned face a look of tantalising piquancy which was enhanced by the beguiling curve of soft lips when she smiled and gibed, 'You've got it all mapped out, haven't you? What I'm allowed to do; where I'm allowed to go; with whom and when! Well, I'm sorry to disappoint you, but if I can't choose for myself, then I'll stay at home!' An emphatic nod reinforced her decision until she saw his teeth clench and his eyes narrow with ominous intent, whereupon she hastily enquired, 'Or—or isn't that acceptable either?' but in such an indeterminate tone that every degree of goading was lost.

His eyes flickered over her briefly. 'I think you already know the answer to that!' he bit out tersely. 'But one thing I will promise you . . . if you're not ready by the time we're due to leave this evening, then I'll come into that room of yours and damned well dress you myself, blue eyes!'

'You wouldn't dare!' but without too much conviction.

'Wouldn't I?' Mark drawled, brows expressively aslant. 'I think we both know better than that, so I wouldn't advise you to put it to the test.'

Shannon didn't think she should either. In fact, the vivid mental pictures his threat conjured up had her lowering her head self-consciously. It was hard enough at the best of times attempting to control her wayward emotions in the face of his sensuous male attraction, without having to contend with the thought of any intimate physical contact as well. Her one previous experience had shown her all too clearly just how vulnerable she was where Mark Seymour's intoxicating touch was concerned.

Lunch was a relaxed and pleasant meal with greetings called to friends and acquaintances, introductions made to those who stopped for brief conversations, and everyone recounting to each other the exhibits that had caught their eye or could prove beneficial to the station. Jane and Davey proudly displayed the contents of the sample bags they had persuaded their mother into buying, and Chris vowed she wouldn't be moving from the grandstand during the afternoon because she was positive she had walked a good ten miles that morning.

As it was, they were all only too pleased to keep to the stands during the afternoon's events for the wind was now knifing across the showgrounds in wild, penetrating swathes and giving Shannon further cause to be grateful for the fleecy coat which was managing to ward off the cold far more effectively than her denim jacket could ever have done.

The buck-jumping and bullock ride events were made more hazardous than usual owing to the animals' natural dislike for the wind; making them harder to handle in the chutes and more determined than ever to dislodge their unwanted burdens the minute they came rearing and bucking into the ring. The Tuesday hands fared no better—or worse—than most of their compatriots in the events, although Don did manage to stay on his bullock for the allotted time—Shannon never knew how—but Tony and Trevor came to early grief by only making it a few yards towards the centre of the arena before flying to earth.

As soon as the rodeo events were completed both Mark and Pete took their leave to prepare for the Grand Parade, and half an hour later the first of the long line of animals began to enter the ring. The horses came first, necks arched proudly and flaunting the multi-coloured ribbons with which they were adorned; heavy-maned Shetlands; lightly-built Arabs, sturdy Australian stockhorses; versatile hacks; and even a pair of perfectly groomed Clydesdales.

The next to follow in the line that was beginning its second circle of the arena were the champion cattle; beef shorthorns; black Angus; hump-backed Brahmans; smooth-coated Santa Gertrudis; pale Murray Greys; enormous Charollais; and last, but by no means least, the major beef breed of Australia and the cattle which had achieved such outstanding success in every cattle-producing country in the world – the red and white Herefords, both poll and horned.

Of course it was to the latter group that Shannon's gaze swung and, more particularly, to the leading animal of the breed – Tuesday Park Overlord, stomping placidly along beside Mark, his back covered by a mass of purple as well as red, white and blue ribbons, his head in a leather halter and a controlling rope through the ring in his nose. Not that he appeared to need either, for in true champion style he totally ignored his surroundings, plodding peacefully as if at home in his own paddock. Even to Shannon's inexperienced eye he was a superior specimen; it was there in the conformation, the scale and the depth, and she almost missed the rest of the entries as they paraded in front of the stand because she couldn't drag her glance from him—or his handler, she admitted ruefully to herself.

After that everything else was an anti-climax, except for a pair of Angora goats which caught the crowd's laughing attention when they began bounding and pulling to show their dislike of being led, and once the lead horses came to the centre of the ring the slowly moving circles of animals halted while the spectators showed their appreciation of such a display of livestock, and then the directions were reversed and one by one the handlers led their charges from the arena and back to their stalls.

The light was just failing by the time they had all made it back to the property, for immediately the parade finished the stock had been carefully loaded for their return as there could be no fast driving for the stockmen with such an important cargo aboard—but once the homestead was reached there began a hectic flurry of activity with the cattle being off-loaded and settled for the night, the house livestock needing to be fed, eggs to be collected, cows to be milked, and everyone vying for the bathroom.

While Chris was bathing and feeding the children, Shannon took the opportunity to search out Tony at the bails. Thankfully she found him alone, waiting for Don to herd the cows in from the paddock, and she crossed the yard swiftly towards him. On seeing her approach he turned in surprise and smiled.

'Hi, have you come to give us a hand?' he asked. 'We were beginning to wonder if you were a jillaroo after all. Ever since your first day here we've never seen you outside working with the stock again.'

Reaching his side, Shannon smiled faintly in return. 'Yes, well, that's—er—another story,' she admitted embarrassedly. 'What I really came to see you about was the dance this evening. I'm sorry, Tony,' she gave him an apologetic look, 'but I'm afraid I won't be able to go with you after all. The *boss* has decreed otherwise!' sarcastically. 'Apparently I'm expected to attend with the family instead. I'm sorry,' she repeated her apology dolefully.

'That's okay, Shannon, no harm done,' he reassured her generously. 'I was rather surprised Mark hadn't already mentioned it to you before I asked this morning—it probably slipped his mind. Still, I'll see you there anyway—just make sure you save some dances for me,' he commanded with a grin.

'Will do,' she returned with an easy smile of her own. 'All of them, if you like. I hardly know anyone else from around these parts.'

'That won't make any difference,' he retorted with feeling. 'No one waits for introductions at the Show dance. I'll be lucky to get a look in once the rest of the mob sets eyes on you.'

'It's not a terribly formal affair, then?'

'Hell, no! It's just an opportunity for everyone to enjoy themselves.'

At this point they were interrupted by an impatient Friesian attempting to push her way past Tony and into the bail where her meal was already in the feed box. Much as she would have liked to have stayed and watched Shannon thought it advisable to return to the homestead to make sure she didn't keep the family waiting, and thus give Mark the chance of carrying out his threat of the morning. So, with a cheery wave to Tony and an acknowledging salute to Don as he urged the rest of the cows into the yard, she hurried back to the brightly lit house.

CHAPTER SEVEN

It was completely dark when Shannon had finished showering, and dressing in a paprika-coloured velvet gown with a square, fitted Empire bodice, the skirt falling in graceful panels to the floor. Standing back to examine herself critically in the mirror, she remembered Mark's comment concerning her slenderness and started to smile. At least she was pleased to see that she could only be described as willowy in the right places! In fact, all in all, she wasn't too unhappy with her appearance tonight.

And nor should she have been, for with the careful application of shadow and mascara the colour of her eyes had deepened in intensity to such an extent they appeared almost violet in the subdued lighting of her bedroom and her soft lips glowed enticingly within their cover of bronze lipstick, giving her a purely female allure which would have been hard to resist.

After attaching a delicate cameo to a black velvet band and fastening it about her throat, she drew a fashionably crocheted and fringed wrap about her shoulders, picked up a golden drawstring evening bag from her bed and stepped out into the hallway.

Chris was coming from the direction of her own room and stopped to inspect Shannon's outfit admiringly.

'Mmm, don't you look good,' she complimented. 'I fear there'll be a few broken hearts in town tomorrow once the local bachelors set their sights on you!'

'I don't know about that,' Shannon laughed. 'I rather think all eyes will be on you tonight. That dress of yours is quite stunning,' she stated sincerely, her eyes taking in the Oriental styled full-length tunic of soft figure flattering creamy beige jersey with its side splits, and chocolate and lemon interwoven embroidery around the high mandarin collar and hem.

'Words guaranteed to lift any young matron's heart,' observed Chris gaily, and linking their arms together. 'Come on, let's see if our dashing escorts are ready and waiting to squire us into town. Davey and Jane are safely ensconced with Mum in her studio, and *I* am looking forward to my last night out on the town before returning home.'

Shannon looked at her in surprise. 'Isn't your mother coming?' she asked.

Chris shook her head negligently. 'No, Mum rarely attends any of these functions. She usually manages to see most of her friends while she's at the Show and would rather spend the evening sketching her impressions while they're still fresh in her mind.'

Shannon digested this in silence, but a somewhat belligerent silence all the same. So—with Chris paired with Pete, and Mark dancing attendance on Hilary Donovan, just what was *she* supposed to do—play gooseberry? What a lovely thought! And her mouth twisted sarcastically as she railed once again at Mark's autocratic decisions which had placed her in such a disagreeable position.

By the time they arrived in town Narrawa Town Hall was ablaze with lights and gaily festooned with banners and award-winning ribbons from both past and present local Shows, as well as intra-state and inter-state ones, which had been won by graziers through the district. The dining tables had been diligently arranged at one end of the long polished floor and decorated with colourful arrangements of fresh and dried flowers, while attentive waiters mingled within the throng of guests dispensing cocktails in long-stemmed glasses, and platters of appetising paté and smoked salmon canapés.

Their wraps removed in the cloakroom, the girls prepared to return to where they could see Mark and Pete conversing with a small group in the crowd, but before they had gone very far Hilary Donovan appeared beside them with a bright and lively smile and Shannon found, to her dismay, that she was uncharitably pleased to note that the other girl's dress of sprigged white brocade didn't really suit her.

'Have you just arrived too?' Hilary stated rather than questioned. 'Looks like being a good evening, doesn't it?' and again continued without waiting for a reply, 'If you're heading in Mark's direction, I'll come with you. From my lowly stature's point of view,' she glanced at the other two girls' greater height wistfully, 'it's just as well he stands out, or it would take me most of the night to wend my way through the crowd looking for him.'

Shannon only vaguely heard Chris making a suitably consoling remark to this confession, for her own eyes had involuntarily gone on ahead to the subject of Hilary's comments. Oh, yes, Mark certainly stood out, she conceded wryly, and it wasn't only because of the fabulous slate blue fine wool suit, cut with a western style yoke and teamed with a navy roll-necked sweater, that he was wearing either. She would have to have been blind not to notice the many admiring and inviting glances being thrown his way by some of the women present—a sure indication she wasn't the only female to experience emotional havoc in the face of his undeniable attraction—and she determined to resist that magnetism with as much willpower as she could bring to bear in an effort to put her feelings back on an even keel.

But when they drew nearer Mark inclined his head towards them and as his slow, lazy look of masculine awareness reached out to her Shannon could feel not only her newly resolved intentions beginning to crumble, but her legs felt close to collapsing too, and in defence she lifted her chin imperceptibly to eye him back defiantly as her last steps brought her to the edge of the group, but his only reaction was an unperturbed smile which took in all three of them and left no doubt in Shannon's mind that her challenges were no more successful and had no more effect upon Mark Seymour than did an irritable steer trying to avoid being mustered. She was a temporary annoyance that would only be allowed as much rein as he permitted before being swiftly and effortlessly put back in her place. Disliking her own thoughts, she hunched her shoulders resentfully and turned her attention to the introductions Pete was making.

Of the five names mentioned it was really only Austin Donovan—Hilary's father—who registered. A short, rotund little man with a ruddy complexion and merry blue eyes, he was an obviously happy-natured individual who enjoyed life to the full and, judging by the frequent beaming glances bestowed in their direction, was fully in accord with the idea of his only daughter becoming the future Mrs Seymour. Accepting a bubbling cocktail from a passing waiter, Shannon staunchly ignored the laughing couple beside her in order to concentrate on what Mr Donovan was saying.

'I heard Mark had employed another jillaroo,' he remarked first, before quizzing interestedly, 'You like the outside work, do you, Shannon?'

A sip from her glass and she answered clearly, almost aggressively, 'Yes! Yes, I do, Mr Donovan. It's varied and far more enjoyable than sitting in a stuffy office all day.' And it would have been too if Mark had given her half a chance!

'I've never employed a jillaroo myself, but with my Hilary showing all the signs of wanting to sample married life in the near future, I guess maybe I ought to be giving it some careful consideration. She's been like another arm to me over the years, and being a widower is a great drawback when it comes to running a property and trying to keep the homestead up to scratch at the same time. If I could just find someone willing to take over some of the household . . .' He tilted his head enquiringly, a twinkle in his blue eyes. 'I don't suppose you'd be interested in changing your employer in return for an increased remuneration, would you, Shannon?' he smiled.

'She would not!' Mark cut in goodhumouredly, and making Shannon wonder if it had been wishful thinking on her part to imagine she detected a certain inflexibility in his voice. 'That's what's called bribery and corruption, Austin. Why don't you advertise for an—er . . .' a significant pause, 'experienced jillaroo if you want one? You never know, you might even be more successful than I was,' he concluded with a taunting smile at Shannon which had her clenching her hand tightly about the stem of her glass in reaction to the double-edged remark.

Now she knew it had been wishful thinking! The only reason Mark didn't want Austin Donovan to tempt her away from Tuesday Park was because he didn't intend to deprive himself of the satisfaction of firing her himself when he no longer had any need of her services. In something akin to despair she drained the last of the liquid in her glass and exchanged it for a full one as another waiter passed. Anyway, what did it matter to her? she shrugged. She was only staying until she had managed to save enough money to give her some small measure of independence, wasn't she? But whatever proprietorial claims Mark might consider he held, she was quite capable, and to her mind more than entitled, to reply to Austin's offer herself, and so she smiled at him appreciatively.

'At least I should be allowed to thank you for your complimentary proposition, Mr Donovan,' she said sincerely. 'It's always nice to know there's a congenial post in the offing if the one you presently hold should for some unknown reason'—a steady, challenging look at Mark—'happen to fall through.'

Mark ignored her glance and started to laugh. 'I'm getting the distinct impression she's playing us off against each other, Austin,' he cautioned the older man lightly.

'I am not!' Shannon denied quickly, heatedly, not wishing Hilary's father to believe that had been the motivation behind her comment.

'No, I'm sure you weren't, lass,' Austin hastened to reassure her cheerfully. 'Mark was only teasing—he knows I wouldn't deliberately set out to steal any of his staff. In a community such as ours we depend upon one another too much to cause bad feeling by purloining our neighbours' employees.'

'Satisfied?' Mark mocked laconically.

That Austin wouldn't deliberately entice anyone in to his employ—yes! That Mark had only been teasing—no! But now was not the time to argue the point, and taking another mouthful of chilled wine she lifted one shoulder negligently and a grudging, 'I guess so,' was finally allowed.

During the last part of their three-way exchange Pete had begun to accompany Chris and Hilary towards the tables at the far end of the hall, but he swung round now to call to Mark, 'I think they're about ready to serve dinner. We'll see you down there—okay?'

Mark accepted the information with a casually raised

hand. 'Right, Pete, we'll be with you in a minute.' Then, 'You coming, Austin?'

'Also in a minute,' that man smiled. 'First, I had better pay my respects to Mrs Toland—I don't think I've seen her since the dance last year. I'll join you shortly,' excusing himself and heading briskly towards a dispersing group on the other side of the room.

Suddenly finding herself alone with Mark, Shannon immediately set off for the tables, but a seemingly courteous hand found her arm and the implacable grip had her slowing her steps considerably and taking another confidence-boosting sip of her cocktail.

'I think you'd better give that a rest until you've had something to eat,' Mark proposed idly, yet at the same time dictatorially relieving her of the glass and placing it on a small table as they passed.

'Why?' Shannon slanted angry blue eyes upwards at the arbitrary action. 'Are you afraid I'm going to disgrace the name of Tuesday Park by passing out under the table halfway through the evening?'

'No, that's not what I'm afraid of, blue eyes. But there is a somewhat turbulent look about you tonight that doesn't augur well for a frictionless evening if mixed with too much alcohol,' he rejoined drily.

'In which case, it might have been better if you'd allowed me to partner Tony as originally planned,' with pointed acerbity.

'You think so?' in ironic scepticism. 'It would appear you've forgotten it's also my responsibility to see to the interests of my senior jackaroo—as well as the junior jillaroo—and Tony's too easy-going to have a hope in hell of restraining you tonight.'

'But you think you can?' the wine dared her to challenge caustically.

He smiled slowly, captivatingly, but Shannon wouldn't, or couldn't, let his apparent sureness go uncontested and, with a reckless shine to her eyes beneath their fringe of dark lashes, she countered scornfully, 'I wouldn't be too confident if I were you, Mr Seymour. After all, it has been known for even the lowliest of workers to rebel—and quite successfully too, I might add—against their employers before now.'

Mark's ensuing laughter had many a thoughtful eye turned their way and it was all Shannon could do to listen to what he was saying when one long forefinger tilted her chin slightly and he advised, 'And it's also not unknown for some employers to come down extremely heavily on those rebellious workers who aren't quite so successful.'

In defence, for her breathing had become a trifle ragged at his casual touch, she pulled her head away sharply and resorted to insolence.

'Ah, yes, the *gate*! It's still there waiting for me, isn't it?' Her hands linked together demurely, but the set of her head belied the pensive expression on her face. 'I wonder if I should treat myself to a dress rehearsal by positioning myself outside it with a suitcase at the ready, as it were? You know, just to get the feel of what it will be like so I'm prepared when your big day finally arrives!'

'You'll be getting the feel of something entirely different if you ride me too hard, blue eyes,' he warned with a deceptively lazy drawl. 'Now, behave yourself,' with an admonishing shake, 'and see if you can't sheath those claws of yours for the rest of the evening before you scratch too deep for your own good, hmm?'

Shannon gave an exaggerated sigh. 'You mean I should purr continuously instead? How unimaginative!'

'But restful,' he murmured chaffingly before seeing her seated next to Chris and moving to the seat beside Hilary at the head of the table laid for six.

So Austin and his daughter were members of their party too, Shannon noted with uncustomary asperity, and immediately pulled herself up short. They were both likeable, friendly people and she found it hard to explain, or even understand, her unreasonable feeling of disappointment upon seeing Mark bending his head intently to listen to what Hilary was saying to him.

What earthly reason could she have for constantly trying to find fault with Hilary Donovan? She didn't normally have trouble in getting along with members of her own sex, but then—she forced herself to accede candidly—neither did she usually react to her employers as she did to Mark. Perhaps the two were tied together in her mind and she was letting the ungovernable antagonism she felt towards Mark unfairly spill over on to his girl-friend?

Now that she had carefully arranged these thoughts, Shannon determinedly set out to be a pleasant table companion—she had no wish for any of the others to guess just how forcibly she resented Mark's command that she accompany them—and when Austin joined them a short time later, and the various courses were being served, she made herself participate in the lighthearted talk that flowed to and fro across the table and, at those times when the conversation veered around to pastoral pursuits, listened with a very genuine interest.

A selection of wines was provided with each dish and after Shannon had pleasurably spooned her way through a delicious seafood cocktail; attentively disposed of mouthwatering tournedos Parisienne, the circle-tied fillet steak garnished with asparagus tips and creamy Béarnaise sauce; and savoured the unbelievably light mocha soufflé, she decided to forgo the sweet-tasting liqueurs and brandy offered with a platter of assorted cheeses, and concluded her meal with a small cup of strong black coffee.

'And what did you think of our Show, Shannon?' Austin asked from her left-hand side once everyone had been served their after-dinner drinks and he had just put a flame to the tip of her cigarette.

'I enjoyed it very much,' she returned earnestly. 'It was

the first country show I've attended and I was surprised at the number of exhibits. There were many more than I expected.'

'If it's exhibits you want to see, then you should get Mark to take you down to one of the big field days the next time he goes,' he suggested helpfully. 'That's where you'll really see the equipment that's available in the industry, and with the comparison strip demonstrations it certainly makes it easier to see and judge for yourself just what some of those machines are capable of doing.'

Shannon nodded. 'That sounds like a good idea,' she agreed.

Not that she had any hope of Mark taking her anywhere to see anything connected with the profession she had attempted to embark upon. If it had been a new dishwasher, or some other associated appliance, she might have had a chance. She permitted herself a small smile. Even then she wouldn't be too confident!

Pete, who had been casually listening to their conversation, now looked down the table to his brother. 'Are you going to the Field Days this year, Mark?' he asked.

Mark broke off what he had been saying to Chris, a thoughtful crease furrowing his forehead. 'I haven't decided yet. Why?'

'Well, Austin was just saying that he thought it would be a good chance for Shannon to see what goes on, and it is quite an experience. Shannon's all for it,' Pete divulged benevolently.

'Is she?'

A laconically lifting eyebrow had Shannon quickly averting her face and drawing sharply on her cigarette while she silently cursed Pete for having added that last comment. Why couldn't he have left well enough alone? Her reply to Austin had only been perfunctory—not expectant!

Now Mark's continuing, 'Well, when I've made my decision I'm sure Shannon and I will be able to come to some suitable arrangement,' had her shifting uncomfortably on her chair, humiliated by the thought that Pete had inadvertently given his brother yet another opportunity to unconditionally prohibit any likelihood of her gaining experience as a jillaroo while in his employ.

She didn't have to strain her mental processes to know what Mark had meant by his 'some suitable arrangement'. If, and when, he decided to go, one Shannon Marshall definitely and categorically would not be included in his plans!

Pete apparently hadn't read his brother's answer in the same way however, for now he sent her an encouraging wink across the table, for which she had some difficulty in raising a smile in response, but it must have looked more sincere than it felt, for he obviously saw nothing amiss and smiled broadly back, thinking the matter all settled in her favour.

The quintet which had been providing the relaxing background music to the hum of dinner chatter now changed to a rather more lively tempo, and thankful for the chance to escape from what, to Shannon at least, had become the disconcerting tension at the table, she accepted Austin's offer to dance with alacrity, putting out her cigarette swiftly and following him eagerly on to the dance floor.

Her steps matched his easily and with Austin being the natural conversationalist that he was, Shannon soon found some of her chagrin dissipating as she concentrated on what her partner was saying, only once having it revived disagreeably when she happened to see Mark and Hilary move into each other's arms as they joined the swelling crowd of dancers.

Resolutely she turned her head away and allowed the wine she had consumed earlier to inspire a sparkling animation to show she hadn't a care in the world, and was totally oblivious to the veiled looks of envy that Austin was receiving and the unusual number of couples who vouchsafed greetings while they circled the floor.

Halfway through the next number Austin was grandiosely tapped on the shoulder by Pete when he moved up beside them, and with a twinkling smile of understanding relinquished his partner to the younger man and danced away with a chuckling Chris.

'Can't have the older generation monopolising you all evening,' grinned Pete as, by mutual agreement, they quickened their steps to a more modern series of movements. 'What did you think of my strategy for getting you to the Field Days? Good, huh?'

Shannon wrinkled her nose impudently. 'That remains to be seen,' she half laughed.

'Why?' Pete sounded surprised. 'I thought Mark's answer was almost as good as an assurance.'

'Did you?' somewhat sardonically.

'If he does go and you are really interested, he'll take you, you know,' he tried to impress upon her seriously.

Somehow Shannon doubted that, but she pretended to be swayed by Pete's greater positiveness and gave him a lightly shrugged, 'You could be right,' before abruptly changing the subject and asking him which one of those present was his 'waylaying' girl-friend.

At first he didn't grasp her meaning. 'My what?' he frowned.

'When you picked me up at the station on my first day here, you said you had been—er—waylaid in town,' she reminded him with a teasing grin. 'I was just wondering which of the girls here was she.'

'Oh, you mean Kay—Kay Youngman,' he laughed across the intervening space, his face clearing. 'As a matter of fact she isn't coming tonight. If my calculations are correct, she should be enjoying a well-deserved day's layover in New York at the moment.'

'She's an air hostess?'

'Uh-huh! Which doesn't exactly give her much time at home.'

'And my arrival cut short your time together when she was in Narrawa. I'm sorry,' she commiserated with him unreservedly.

'Hey, there's no need to look so downhearted about it. We're not *that* serious about one another,' he grinned at her doleful expression.

Shannon held his gaze steadily for a few moments and then started to laugh. 'Oh, isn't that just like a man!' she taunted. 'Here I am, picturing you pining for your long-lost love, and you ... you couldn't care less! All you're interested in doing is having a good time.'

'Well, I expect Kay's doing exactly the same,' he grinned excusingly. 'It's not as if we've made any eternal vows, or anything like that,' in hasty assurance.

She gave him a mock, narrow-eyed interrogation. 'So *you* say!'

Catching hold of her hand Pete whirled her around energetically, bringing her to a halt close against his chest with both arms wrapped tightly about her.

'And what about you while we're on the subject, little matchmaker?' he took in her startled face with a laugh. 'How do we know you haven't someone loyally awaiting your return in Sydney while you're insouciantly setting our tranquil locale on its proverbial ear, hmm?'

'I *have* not—and I *am* not!' Shannon contradicted his suggestions in order.

Pete shook his head knowingly. 'Don't you believe it! Have you any idea the number of comments your presence has raised tonight?'

'Such as ...?' she openly disbelieved.

'Such as ... where does she come from? ... what's she doing up here? ... and, in the case of most of the single blokes ... how do we hire one like her? I think just about every grazier from here to the Queensland border is contemplating employing one of your sisters-in-occupation at the moment.'

The incongruity of the situation appealed to the humorous side of Shannon's nature, bringing a twinkle to her eyes and a chuckle to her throat. If they only knew! She speculated amusedly as to what their individual reactions would be if they did, indeed, find they had hired 'one like her'. Much the same as Mark's, probably—instant dismissal—she concluded with sobering insight.

'What caused that rapid change of expressions?' Pete immediately enquired interestedly.

Shannon shrugged her shoulders lightly. 'Oh, nothing,' she dismissed the query airily, although she rapidly followed it with an evading, 'But I think you'd better take your arms away, Pete,' recalling the manner in which he was still holding her. 'In case you haven't noticed, we're on the receiving end of some very jaundiced looks while we're shuffling around like this, and not the least of which,' as a certain couple came into view, the man's smile being supplanted by a cool raking scrutiny, 'is coming from your brother ... my boss!' she grimaced.

'So? Let him look, he's probably only jealous,' with a brotherly disregard which Shannon, unfortunately, couldn't share and she asserted positively, 'That I very much doubt!' before continuing, 'But in any case ...'

Before she could complete what she had been about to say an authoritative hand descended on to Pete's shoulder and with a rueful grin creasing his face he turned to Mark resignedly.

'Knew it wouldn't be long before someone cut in. I'm surprised I lasted this long,' he said, and with a friendly tweak to one of Shannon's curls he had changed partners and was swinging Hilary away without giving anyone else a chance to speak.

Embarrassed by Pete's assumption as to the reason for

his brother's cutting in, Shannon kept her head bent and hunched one shoulder defensively.

'I'm sorry,' she murmured awkwardly. 'Pete didn't realise ...' Another shrug. 'He thought you cut in because you wanted to dance with me.'

'And don't I?' came the rather amused-sounding question from somewhere above her head, making Shannon raise her eyes experimentally, but only for a moment, and then lower them again to the region of his chest.

'Only as an expected duty,' she acknowledged quietly.

Not until he had captured one of her hands and inexorably pulled her into his arms, their steps picking up the beat of the music automatically, did Mark bend his head close beside her temple to quizz disquietingly, 'Am I supposed to interpret that as meaning you would rather it was for some other reason?'

Temporarily Shannon found herself immersed in a seething mass of disturbing thoughts as a result of this evocative inference, but with a violent shake of her head she hotly disclaimed the suggestion with a swift, 'No! Of course not!' followed by an explanatory, 'I just meant that, having been more or less pushed into it by Pete, neither of us really had much choice.'

'Then why *do* you think I cut in?'

To dispel the last of her capricious mental images Shannon retorted truthfully, but ironically, 'I didn't know you actually had! I was under the impression you'd only interrupted us in order to complain.'

'About what?'

'Who knows?' she returned flippantly, irritated by what she considered to be his deliberate stalling. 'Does the boss ever need any particular reason? I would have thought my continuing presence here was cause enough!'

If it had been her intention to annoy then it seemed she had succeeded, because the grasp on her hand tightened noticeably and she was advised peremptorily, 'Stop trying to be cute, blue eyes, or I might think you're discomfited by a guilty conscience!'

Increasingly aware that she was forcing a showdown she would rather have avoided, Shannon still couldn't forestall the rush of goading words from her lips and, denying the truth of his allegation when she had already rebuked Pete for the same thing, she gibed recklessly, 'You surprise me! I wasn't aware girls like me were supposed to have a conscience—guilty, or otherwise!' and finished with the ambivalent demand, 'What have I done that I should feel guilty about, anyway?'

'As if you don't already know, you equivocating little cat!' His words reached out to her unhurriedly, each one resounding coldly against her ears and spreading fingers of ice along her veins at the undisguised contempt in his tone. 'But as you appear so determined to have it out in the open, then it will be my pleasure to accommodate you, because although your blatantly exhibitionist mode of dancing was, no doubt, very much appreciated by Guy Crawford in the past, I flatly refuse to tolerate an employee of mine providing such a promiscuous display for the sheer hell of demonstrating just how sensuous she can become with only a little alcoholic persuasion! *That* clear enough for you?' he grated remorselessly.

Inarticulately Shannon could only just hold the hostile amber gaze directed so forcefully at her and catch her breath in a series of choking swallows as the biting words penetrated. The previous hectic colour ebbed rapidly from her face, leaving it white and strained with only two sapphire eyes shimmering with a hint of unshed tears to offset its pallor until her own anger surged to the surface, bringing with it a return of a more natural tint to her creamy skin.

That his merciless denunciation should have been more fairly consigned to his own brother she had no intention of demeaning herself by so informing him. Instead she at-

tempted to wrench herself haughtily out of his grip, but
when this failed flung up her head defiantly, the effort
behind the uncaring smile that caught at her mouth making
her facial muscles ache unbearably.

'Oh, absolutely, boss ... absolutely,' she ventured to
confirm facetiously. 'But now, if you have no—no objections ...' the strain was beginning to tell and her simulated
nonchalance starting to crack, 'I—I think I'd rather return
to the table and sit the rest of this one out.'

Her initial movement towards that end was halted in
mid-stride by Mark's unrelenting hand firming against her
back and his hold on her fingers increasing when she would
have pulled away.

'As it so happens, I do object, blue eyes,' he informed her
evenly. 'If you don't like being chastised for your actions
then I might suggest you give more careful consideration
before indulging those ardent responses of yours in future.'

Hurt by his pitiless censures, Shannon's one desire was to
strike back—and just as derogatorily. With as much disdain
as she could gather she met his disapproving glance without
so much as a wince.

'Oh, it's not your hypercriticism that's bugging me,' she
lied flagrantly. 'Rather it's the idea of being forced to dance
with you when I have no desire to do so. Up until *now*, I've
always found dancing to be a pleasure,' she added insolently with a slighting half smile.

'And judging by your previous performance tonight, a
physically gratifying one at that.'

Much to Shannon's surprise and annoyance, Mark
seemed not one whit put out by her attempts to snub and
merely afforded her a smooth and arrogant smile—for all
the world as if she had placed her smarting resentment on
display—and completely disregarded her stormy vexation
as evidenced by the angle of a challenging chin and the
flash of arresting blue eyes, which eventually goaded her to
taunt wildly with a self-maligning inelegance normally for-

eign to her nature, 'What's up, Mark? You wouldn't happen to be suffering from a bad case of sour grapes because your girl-friend isn't the same way inclined, would you?'

Shannon didn't need the bruising pressure of Mark's fingers on hers to let her know she had gone too far. One appalled glance at the savage fury closing over his face was quite sufficient to send uncontrollable shivers of apprehension down her spine, put a hesitating falter in her footsteps, and have her chewing at her lip with misgiving.

Without meeting his eyes she immediately regretted with a low penitence, 'I—I'm sorry, I . . .'

'Don't bother! I doubt you even know the meaning of the word!' The rebuff lashed over her bowed head with a cutting contempt. 'In fact, I strongly recommend you adhere to a strict self-preserving silence where I'm concerned for the rest of the evening, Shannon, because if you throw down the gauntlet just once more, so help me, I refuse to accept the onus for the backlash!' he counselled harshly.

Shannon opened her mouth to reiterate her apologies, but closed it again without having uttered a word upon seeing the forbidding look in Mark's eyes and nodded her head miserably in acknowledgment of his warning. The band had ceased playing during the course of his condemnation and now it was with a heaved sigh of relief that she felt herself being ushered back to the table with a swift, efficient stride that all too clearly showed his hard disciplined anger and eagerness to be rid of her unwanted company.

Cursorily seated, Shannon withdrew a nerve soothing cigarette from her bag and gratefully accepted a light from Austin Donovan, knowing how visibly unsteady her own hands would have been had she performed this task for herself, but even so it wasn't until some minutes had passed that she could feel her mercurial emotions subsiding into place and she could join in the conversations flowing about her with any shade of normalcy.

However, it was still with a fervent willingness, out of all proportion to the actual pleasure his presence engendered, that she assented to Tony's offer to dance once he had struck an undeviating course for their table as soon as he had passed through the imposing cedar doors leading into the increasingly crowded hall.

'Missed me?' was his first teasing query as their steps took them side by side into the routine of the Bus Stop.

Shannon's eyes turned ceilingwards. 'You don't know the half of it!' she endorsed wryly.

'Sounds promising ... or did you find dining out under the watchful eye of the boss just a little too deterring for total enjoyment?'

'Er—you could say that,' she admitted, carefully tongue-in-cheek, but adding with more spirit, 'It's demoralising enough him waiting to criticise everything I do at the homestead, without having to endure the same treatment in my free time as well!'

Tony looked sideways at her interestedly. 'You know, there's something going on around here that intrigues me,' he confessed with a smile. 'This wouldn't have anything to do with your not working with the stock on the property, would it?'

An indecisive movement of her hands and a rueful grimace were all Shannon gave in way of an answer and Tony pounced on her non-committal actions discerningly.

'Come clean, Shannon,' he adjured encouragingly. 'The fact that you were hired as a jillaroo, as well as home help, and apart from your first day you haven't once been seen working outside the homestead hasn't gone unnoticed, you know.'

'I suppose it was too much to expect it not to give rise to speculation of one sort or another,' she sighed.

'So...?'

'So I was fired on my first day for not being what I was supposed to be,' she disclosed impulsively in headlong fashion.

Tony's forehead knitted uncomprehendingly. 'You've lost me somewhere,' he half grinned. 'If you weren't supposed to be a jillaroo, what were you supposed to be?'

'But that's just it,' Shannon explained patiently, drily. 'I *was* supposed to be a jillaroo, but I've never been one before and that's what caused all my trouble. I *wasn't* experienced in the work like I claimed to be.'

A ready grin of realisation began to pull at Tony's mouth. 'So that's why you were all fingers and thumbs that first day,' he laughed. 'But what on earth made you try a deception like that on someone of Mark Seymour's stamp? You were bound to be caught out,' he added unnecessarily.

'Now he tells me!' joked Shannon with satirical feeling, her eyebrows lifting explicitly. 'Where were you when that small piece of advice might have done some good?'

He laughed again. 'But if the boss fired you, how come you're still at the station? I would have thought an attempted ruse of that order would have been enough to have you packed off back to where you came from ... and on the double at that.'

'Which is exactly where I was headed until it was found that Chris had already made arrangements to fly home next week which, fortunately for me, left the Seymours without a housekeeper.'

'So you'll be taking over in the homestead when she leaves?'

After her last demolishing clash with Mark, Shannon couldn't have said with any conviction that she still had a job at all—let alone one where she was nominally in charge—but as she didn't envisage relating all of her problems to Tony she merely shrugged lightly and agreed, 'That's the arrangement,' before her expression turned wistful and she reluctantly admitted, 'Although I still wish I could learn something about the livestock while I'm here.'

'Well, that's no problem,' Tony promptly came to her aid. 'I can teach you in any spare time you get.'

A hopeful light shone in Shannon's eyes and then died. 'Thanks, Tony, I'd love to, but,' she wrinkled her nose disconsolately, 'I'm under a strict ultimatum to never again lay a finger on any of the boss's precious stock.'

Tony tried to smother his laughter, but couldn't subdue it altogether. 'Not that I can honestly say I blame him,' he smiled broadly. 'Though I doubt he meant every animal on the place. After all, everyone has to start somewhere and learning how to milk a cow and ride a horse are usually first on the list in any jackaroo's indoctrination—that is, if he can't already do both—so I can't see why you shouldn't start on the same,' he reasoned plausibly.

'My sentiments entirely,' she smiled. 'But I bet Mark won't agree, all the same.'

'Then I suggest we don't tell him,' out of the corner of his mouth in his most conspiratorial manner.

'Oh, lord, no!' Shannon vetoed the idea swiftly with a horrified gasp.

'There would be the devil to pay when he found out, and it's not fair to involve you in my troubles too. I'm sure he'd have no qualms about sacking the pair of us! Besides, didn't you just say Mark Seymour wasn't the type of man to try and deceive?'

'Sure, for something like you intended, but I hardly think this could be classified on the same level and there's not much chance of him finding out anyway. Don and I are usually back earlier than the others in order to do the milking, and from the bails you get a good view of anyone approaching the homestead, so there's no worry there. As for learning to ride—well, Mark's often away for a day or so at a time . . .' He let the words trail off invitingly.

A moment's consideration and, 'The others?' Shannon queried hesitantly, not wanting to commit herself completely.

'Don't worry about them—they're not likely to give us away,' he offered cheerfully. 'It's the type of work they would expect you to be doing as a jillaroo.'

Outwardly Shannon was all for the idea. Inwardly she was shaking just a little with trepidation, but it was this very trepidation that finally made up her mind for her. Why shouldn't she gain some experience? What harm could she possibly do with someone there to teach her? Wasn't that the reason she had applied for the position?—to learn all she could about a jillaroo's life—and if she wasn't taught now she would never be able to apply for a like post. She nodded her head decisively.

'All right—I'm game, if you are!'

'Now we're getting somewhere,' Tony commended happily. 'Just let me know when you're ready for your first lessons and you'll be on your way.'

'I hope you don't mean that literally,' she misinterpreted his words with a shuddering laugh. 'But, in any case, I doubt whether I'll have the time before Chris leaves because we'll have to cram in as many driving lessons as possible if I'm to have a hope of getting a licence before next weekend. However, from there on,' she grinned impishly, 'I'll be dogging your footsteps in an effort to gain as much experience as I possibly can. In fact, before very long, you'll probably be sick to death of me always hanging around in your every spare moment.'

'That I very much doubt,' he disallowed with an admiring glance.

When the next interval came in the music and Tony would have escorted her back to the table, Shannon demurred with a shake of her head and followed him back to the long gleaming bar instead, where they pulled themselves up on to adjacent stools and she tried hard to dismiss Mark from her troubled thoughts. Accepting a thirst-quenching lemon drink from Tony, she forced herself to put on a carefree front and refused to permit her glance to slide, even momentarily, towards the table she had left behind.

Nevertheless, after another two dances with Tony and a

couple with complete strangers, she reluctantly decided she couldn't prolong her absence any longer without appearing unbearably rude to the other members of the Seymour party, and with dragging footsteps allowed Tony to usher her in that direction as the band prepared to launch into another number.

Amazingly enough, though, she found that during her absence from Mark's ever watchful presence she had, at last, somehow managed to erect something of a barrier against the head-to-toe appraisal coming her way from cool eyes as she resumed her seat amidst Tony's pleasantries to the rest of the group and, in consequence, she was thankful to be able to return the dispassionate regard composedly before turning and replying to a remark Chris made.

From there on the evening seemed to pass intolerably slowly for Shannon as, even while dancing, she couldn't seem to prevent her wilful thoughts from straying back to Mark, and the overwhelming effect he appeared to have on her. Of course he was a powerfully attractive man, but surely that wasn't sufficient reason for her to be on the defensive all the time, was it? Disconcertingly too, he had the uncanny ability to bring out the worst in her and, as she was normally a very even-tempered person, this was also giving her some cause for concern. All in all, she decided moodily, her venture into station life hadn't proved too successful—or satisfying—so far.

CHAPTER EIGHT

As Shannon had foreseen, the remaining days before Chris's departure for the Gulf were hectic ones. There were driving lessons galore, as well as questions regarding the rules of the road from both Chris and Pete until she was at least carefully capable of obtaining her licence, if not masterfully efficient in doing so.

A full day was spent in Narrawa with Chris advising her at which stores the property had accounts for the purchase of their bulk provisions and the carriers used for delivering the goods to the homestead, as well as ordering the next three months' supplies so that Shannon could start off with a well-stocked pantry.

More hours were occupied by Chris replenishing her family's wardrobes and purchasing a various assortment of presents and knick-knacks, most of which were to be freighted north in order that she didn't exceed her luggage allowance on the plane.

The greater part of Thursday, and Friday morning, was spent in packing and making sure nothing had been left behind, interspersed here and there with Chris's personal hints and tips regarding the running of the household as they came to mind, so that all there was left to do Friday afternoon was to say a fond farewell before Mark drove her and the children into town to catch the plane to Brisbane on the first leg of their long journey which would see them covering the more than fifteen hundred-kilometre flight to Mount Isa the next morning, where a day-and-a-half visit was planned with friends before flying east to Cloncurry early the following Monday and meeting up with Chris's husband, Paul, who would pilot them the rest of the way in their own light aircraft.

Chris's leaving appeared to have been the signal the

weather had been waiting for, as on the following days the temperature began slowly dropping while the winds howled across the plateau and through the valleys with a buffeting ferocity that had proud trees bending their heads low in obeisance and scurried defenceless clouds whimsically beneath an ashen sky. And many times had Shannon been thankful for the warmth of her sheepskin jacket when, leaving a prepared dinner simmering on the range, she had slipped out of the house in the deepening dusk to help and learn from Tony and Don at the bails.

Within a few days she had eased into a routine of her own regarding the running of the homestead and with only Mrs Seymour and herself at home most days found it considerably less arduous than when she had been looking after her father and holding down a job at the same time in the city.

This particular morning she had decided to see whether she could make some headway in tidying the papers and correspondence that lay strewn over the desk, as well as being piled haphazardly in a wire tray on the top of the filing cabinet, in Mark's office.

Tentatively at first—she wasn't sure Mark would approve, or even appreciate her efforts to restore a sense of orderliness to the room—but more positively as time passed and she had convinced herself that he couldn't possibly prefer to work with such chaos surrounding him. After twice stumbling over a battered old tin box occupying a central space beside his chair, she pushed it into one corner and began rummaging through the filing drawers in an attempt to locate the correct folders for the pile of letters she had gathered together and which, judging by the scrawled comments thereon, had already received replies.

Among the odds and ends that defied placement there were a number of photographs; some yellow and fading with age, but others of a more recent vintage, and when one fluttered to the floor she bent to retrieve it and stood carefully scanning the laughing faces depicted.

It was a class photo—she had immediately recognised the tiny Seymour Vale schoolhouse—or, perhaps for that reason, she deduced with a smile, it should probably be classified as a school photo, for it contained children whose ages spanned the whole range of the primary group. Her eyes were drawn instantly to a boy of about eleven seated in the centre of the front row and holding a large trophy in his hands, while the girl beside him happily flaunted a laurel-wreathed cup.

'What's keeping you so interested, eh?'

The question spoken so unexpectedly had Shannon jumping in surprise and whirling round in flustered embarrassment, brought on as much by the fact that Mark had caught her inspecting a photo of himself so closely as by the idea that he could construe her action as prying into things which were none of her business. Doubly watchful, she moved defensively and thrust the print towards him.

'I'm sorry, but it fell on the floor. I wasn't meaning to be inquisitive.'

His mouth crooked slightly, laconically. 'Nobody suggested you were,' he said as his glance ranged over the room, taking note of every change she had made, Shannon didn't doubt. Then, 'Did you do all this?'

There was no indication in either his tone or expression as to whether he was pleased or otherwise with her unsolicited interference with his business methods, so Shannon took the line of least resistance.

'I'm sorry ... I guess the secretary in me must have been crying out to be appeased,' she excused her actions protectively.

Interested eyes came to rest on the guarded face before him as Mark leant back lazily against the desk, hands resting lightly on the top on either side of lean hips, long legs stretched comfortably before him.

'Is that what you were before you decided to become

a—um—jillaroo?' he wanted to know.

Stung by the thread of satire she detected in his query, Shannon sent him one baleful glare before giving a terse, 'Yes,' in reply.

Under other circumstances she might have been tempted to add more, but as their relationship had deteriorated to one of almost monosyllabic sparsity since their confrontation at the dance she was extremely hesitant about impairing it further.

Now, as he still hadn't voiced his opinion in respect of her morning's work, she moved restlessly and turned for the door, but his next proposition had her jerking back to face him once more.

'Aren't you going to finish it?' he asked softly.

'I didn't know if you'd want me to,' she admitted candidly. 'I thought you might have been annoyed because I'd...'

She broke off in heart-stopping turmoil when Mark began to smile, feeling her face grow warm and her breath become uneven in response to the heavy beating of her heart. It was the first real smile he had actually given her and, from Shannon's point of view, the result was disastrous!

'And my being annoyed would have worried you?' he taunted mildly, disbelievingly.

'Well, of course, it would,' Shannon retorted edgily, upset for permitting herself to succumb so adolescently to the effect of one male smile. 'I was only trying to help.'

'For which I'm very grateful,' he owned freely, easing away from the desk and moving with fluid grace into the partnering padded leather chair. 'I'm sorry to say that ever since our previous housekeeper left to look after her widowed sister, the office work has been allowed to get rather much out of hand. She had had some clerical experience in her youth and used to help out with the filing and such when she could,' he explained.

'If you had just filed the letters you'd replied to, it wouldn't have been in half the mess,' Shannon chided sweetly, enjoying being able to reprove him for a change.

Not that it seemed to worry Mark, for he merely gave an acknowledging grin and dipped his head. 'I might have done had we not been so busy over the last few months. Besides, isn't that women's work?' he finished on a goading note.

Shannon's eyes widened indignantly. 'How nice to know we're good for *something*!' she retaliated speedily.

'Oh, I'm sure there's a number of things you're good for,' he half smiled.

'But—apart from doing the filing, of course—not one that you can think of right now!'

'I wouldn't exactly say that,' Mark countered drily, leaving her in no uncertainty as to what his thoughts might be as his eyes travelled her slender length slowly and came to rest disquietingly on softly parted lips.

Try as she might Shannon couldn't stand passively under that intensely provoking regard, and any ideas she might have had of passing it off indifferently were quickly destroyed within the first few seconds by her own flushing betrayal of the senses, so that she was left with no alternative but to refuse to answer and thereby deny him another chance to perturb her.

Dropping her gaze to the pile of photos on the desk, she enquired throatily, 'Where would you like me to put these? I—I wasn't sure before,' while painstakingly squaring them into a neat pile.

A large tanned hand came into her line of vision and closed over her nervously active fingers, relieving them of the prints and placing them beside the telephone.

'At the moment I suggest you leave them just where they are, blue eyes, otherwise you're likely to shuffle the images away altogether, and I have to sort through them for the Centenary Committee yet.'

He sounded amused and the thought rankled. 'I'll do the rest of the mail instead, then,' she snapped, and heading for the filing cabinet hauled open the top drawer angrily, but when next she returned to the desk for another pile of papers it was to find Mark with the old tin box open beside his chair and an even larger collection of photographs gathering on the desk.

Espying the one she had been inspecting when he returned to the office, her curiosity got the better of her, and fingering the photo lightly she probed shyly, 'What were the trophy and cup for?'

Mark leant back and grinned. 'Small Schools' Association awards,' he imparted agreeably. 'The cup for winning the annual general sports, and the trophy for the competitor with the highest individual points. We considered it a great feat at the time—it was the eighth year in succession that the school had won both prizes.'

'Some record,' Shannon conceded with an instinctive smile. 'I suppose that's the kind of thing the committee want for the Centenary display, isn't it?'

'That, and any other memorabilia that depicts life as it's been lived in the area over the last hundred years.'

'Were the Seymours the first to settle the district?' she now asked, somewhat diffidently, not wishing to appear as though her interest was due to any other cause than an historical one.

'One of,' he confirmed negligently. 'Although we're the longest surviving to date—the rest have either died out, or sold out and moved elsewhere.'

She waved a hand towards the wide windows to indicate the neatly fenced paddocks beyond the confines of the homestead.

'I suppose it's changed a great deal since those days too.'

'Uh-huh, quite a lot,' Mark agreed reflectively, as if sensing the wistful regret behind her words. 'Not so much in recent years, of course, but I guess you could say the original settlers would have a hard time recognising most of the region if they were to return today.' He bent down to grasp the tin box which he placed on the front of the desk. 'There's some photographs in there taken in the latter half of last century that would give you some idea of what it used to look like, if you're interested,' he suggested casually.

Pleased as much by Mark's willingness to talk as by his offer to search through photos she knew must be unique and, in some cases, of great historical value, Shannon nodded eagerly, making dark curls bounce on to her forehead which were brushed aside with an expeditious hand.

At her obvious animation Mark smiled lazily. 'You may as well take that seat,' indicating the chair on the other side of the desk, 'and if you come across anything you think might be suitable you can check with me ... okay?'

'You mean, you want me to sort out those I think would qualify for the display?' she queried in astonishment, not quite believing that was what he had meant at all. Up until now she'd had the distinct impression that Mark Seymour didn't trust her to be able to do anything correctly.

'That's right,' he endorsed her enquiry easily, and his mouth tilted disarmingly into an ironic smile. 'It's what's known as passing the buck. You shouldn't have shown such an interest.'

'Oh, I—I don't mind,' Shannon faltered under the effect of that warm gaze. 'I love looking through family albums and cleaning out store rooms—all that sort of thing—it's fascinating the old bits and pieces you find.'

'I shouldn't let anyone else on the committee hear you say that, otherwise you'll more than likely find yourself roped in to help ransack the district for items to go on show.'

'I wouldn't mind that either!' she stated categorically, her shaking head emphasising the point. 'Just think of all the outbuildings there must be around here where people have put things away and forgotten all about them!' warming to the idea.

Mark's eyes held hers intently. 'Are you serious?' he asked.

'Of course!'

'Then you'd better come to the next meeting—another volunteer will be met with open arms—but I warn you, you'll probably find yourself rushed off your feet over the next couple of months. Still want to come?'

'Very much so—I would love to help if I can,' she returned enthusiastically, conveniently convincing herself that her earnestness was purely for the work involved and was not in any way connected to the notion that if she was totally committed to the Centenary then her post at Tuesday would be secure for some time to come. She knew she was still on probation in Mark's eyes with regard to her housekeeping, and the thought that he would one day employ someone permanently for the position still came to worry her in unguarded moments.

Settling down willingly to her task, Shannon became engrossed for the next hour and only occasionally was forced to refer to Mark when the print she was studying had no informative notes penned on its back. One of these was of a slightly built, rather dour-looking woman in a white high-necked blouse, and full skirt of some dark-coloured material, standing beside a giant of a man dressed in moleskins and pale patterned shirt with a kerchief knotted about his throat, and sporting a luxuriant spade-like beard. That the man was a relative of Mark's she didn't dispute. The physique and features were too reminiscent of the man sitting opposite her for Shannon not to have noticed, and she waited interestedly for Mark's answer to her question as to who they were.

A short scrutiny of the photo and, 'That's Daniel Ernest and Georgina Agnes—the first Seymours to settle this property.'

Shannon nodded complacently, her thoughts corroborated. That would probably make the man in the picture Mark's great, or great-great-grandfather. She studied the pair again.

'Georgina doesn't look as if she's exactly enamoured of the life out here, does she?' she pointed out irresistibly, blue eyes twinkling.

The pen Mark was using stopped in mid-sentence and his head lifted slowly. 'You probably wouldn't either if you also had fifteen children by the time you were forty,' he remarked a trifle sardonically.

'*Fifteen!* Good grief!' Shannon's twinkle faded with a gulp, but after another horrified look at the woman under discussion couldn't restrain herself from joking under her breath, 'Didn't she know what was causing it?'

Obviously she hadn't spoken softly enough, for Mark now fixed her with steadfast eyes. 'Why? Don't you like children?' he quizzed.

'Of course I do!' Shannon was quick to defend herself. 'But ... well...' she found herself growing hot and pulled at the collar of her turtle-necked sweater, 'I mean to say, enough is usually enough! She was rather a glutton about it, wasn't she?'

'From necessity rather than choice, I imagine,' Mark commented philosophically. 'Not only because children were a relatively reliable workforce when they grew older, but also to ensure that at least a percentage of them reached maturity. As it was, she lost three from typhoid and one from scarlet fever within a single twenty-four-hour period three years before that picture was taken.'

Shannon's forehead creased with compassion. 'Oh, how dreadful!' she exclaimed. 'No wonder the poor woman looks so sad. Wasn't there a doctor available?'

Broad shoulders lifted resignedly. 'There was one in Narrawa, but as it was a three-day ride to get there at the time, unfortunately, the children had all died before Daniel could return with him.'

'So she couldn't even have her husband with her for support when they died,' Shannon sighed deeply in commiseration. 'She must have been brokenhearted for the rest of her life.'

'No doubt, although from what we know of her she was quite a tartar, and their deaths didn't stop her from ruling the rest of the family with a rod of iron.'

'What, even her husband?' she just had to provoke.

'So they say.'

Gazing at the downbent head as Mark resumed his writing, Shannon found her thoughts rushing onwards and had involuntarily blurted out, 'Well, you certainly wouldn't take after him in that respect, would you?' before she realised she was actually speaking her thoughts aloud, and watched with gathering dismay as Mark replaced the cap on his pen and laid it unhurriedly on the desk before folding strong arms across a chest made even larger by the heavy-knit jumper he was wearing.

'What did you say?' he demanded quietly, but tautly.

Shannon swallowed hard and fumbled unhappily with the rest of the photos in her hands. 'Er—it was nothing important—I was just sort of ... talking to myself,' she tried to pass it off with a shrug.

'Quite possibly,' he conceded with such an arrogant expression that she found it almost impossible to keep her temper in check. 'But as I believe it also concerned myself then I think I'm entitled to hear just exactly what you did say, don't you ... hmm?' with one sarcastically lifting brow.

Being fairly certain he already knew precisely what she had said didn't make it any easier for Shannon to keep her rising emotions under control, but she was still determined to make some sort of effort to avoid bringing the morning's amiability to an end.

'I—well, except for the beard, you do resemble him very closely,' she attempted to reasonably justify her remark.

'So . . .?'

Her mouth set in a mutinous line and her chin angled upwards. If he wasn't prepared to make the effort, why should she?

'So I just couldn't see *you* following in his footsteps and permitting your wife to be anywhere but right under your thumb!' she snapped sarcastically, and completely discarding any previous ideas of pacification.

'Which is, of course, the right and proper place for them to be,' he gibed aggravatingly. 'However, love often makes a man do strange things, which could possibly account for Daniel accepting his wife's behaviour as a form of recompense for the loss of her children, but,' his jaw tightened significantly, 'as I don't happen to *be* married, then you wouldn't have any idea what I might, or might not, be likely to do if I was in love, have you, blue eyes?'

Those very same eyes blazed back at him fiercely. 'Hardly!' she scoffed with a mocking grimace. 'Although with the chauvinistic tendencies you display, it isn't difficult to guess!'

'You mean . . . just as those feminist inclinations of yours leave one in no doubt about *your* ethics?' Mark countered immediately, and proceeded to count them off one by one against his fingers with every evidence of satiric pleasure. 'Conniving—deceiving—lying—argumentative—stubborn—unrepentant and downright aggravating!'

Shannon bit hard at her lip to stop its trembling at his ruthless denunciation, miserably aware that due to her own rash and thoughtless acquiescence to Guy's story she had placed herself in the invidious position where she could not, in all honesty, refute any of Mark's allegations. Not even his accusation that she was unrepentant because, strangely, never once had she regretted coming to Tuesday. However, she still found it impossible to receive his castigation meekly and compelled herself to pout uncaringly.

'Well, I wouldn't be human if I didn't have a few faults, would I?' she quipped, and managed to give a fair imitation of a smile. 'But look who's talking about deception anyway! I didn't notice any hesitancy on your part in pretending to show me over the property on my first day when, in reality, it was just a trap to let me prove how ignorant I was!'

'Which, I might add, you did extremely efficiently,' he drove home the truth adamantly and had Shannon colouring in remembrance. 'And is that what's been riling you all this time, eh? That ... or because I kissed you?'

Caught unawares, Shannon could only stare at him wordlessly, unable to deny that she felt an unconquerable magnetism towards him but shocked to think it could be anything other than a passing attraction.

The vibrant call of the telephone pealing round the room spared her the necessity for any further such disquieting thoughts as Mark bent to answer it, but when, after he had been conversing for only a few seconds, she would have risen from her chair he startled her by holding the receiver towards her saying, 'It's for you,' in a voice she could only describe as glacial.

'For me? Who is it?' making sure her fingers didn't touch his when she took the receiver from him and raised it to her ear.

'Answer, and you'll find out, won't you?'

His sarcastic stock answer was no help and pressing her lips together vexedly Shannon turned away and spoke into the mouthpiece.

'Shannon? Hi, how are things going?' Guy's voice came winging along the wire and with one horrified stare at Mark's stony expression her spirits dropped to an all-time low. Of all the times Guy could have chosen to ring, it would have to be right now, reminding Mark once again of the circumstances surrounding her arrival—not that he ever seemed to need reminding, she amended mournfully.

'Shannon? Are you still there?'

Abruptly she realised she hadn't answered his greeting. 'Yes, yes, I'm here. I'm sorry, Guy, what were you saying?'

'I said ... how are things going up there? Still got them fooled, have you?'

She could almost see him grinning at the other end and her fingers wound agitatedly into the coiled cord of the phone. 'No, I haven't, so please don't joke about it,' she requested unhappily.

'What! Already?' They were expressions of patent disbelief. 'Where did we go wrong?'

'I don't know about you, but I took a header right at the beginning.'

'Poor love,' he sympathised softly. 'I thought Mark sounded a bit cool when he answered the phone. Was he very mad when he found out?'

A *bit* cool! Shannon almost laughed hysterically. Guy either wasn't very perceptive, or else he was trying to make light of it for her benefit. She answered his question drily. 'What do you think?'

'Well, it couldn't have been too bad, otherwise you wouldn't still be there,' he surmised reasonably.

Shannon gulped hollowly. 'Don't you believe it!' she recommended.

'Then how come you are still there?' Guy queried, nonplussed.

Knowing full well that Mark could hear every word she was saying had Shannon hesitating and taking a covert look over her shoulder to where he had taken up his pen and began writing once again. She wished he would leave the room so she might have a proper conversation with Guy. Under the circumstances she was finding it awkward to give only non-committal replies to Guy's questions.

'Shannon! You didn't answer my...' His voice trailed

off and then strengthened again. 'Oh, I get it, Mark's still there with you, is he?'

She nodded into the receiver. 'Now you're getting the idea.'

'Well, never mind, we can have a good talk about it when I come up for the Centenary.'

'You're coming here?' she gasped.

Guy laughed. 'There's no need to sound so stunned about it. You must have realised that as former residents of the district, both my parents and I would be attending the celebrations.'

'But—but ...' she stammered, her mind filled with pictures of the mortifying scene when Mark explained to Mr Crawford what she and Guy had done.

'Good lord, Shannon! Stop sounding so panic-stricken! That's weeks away yet and by that time Mark should well and truly have cooled down. He can't stay mad for ever, you know,' he advised confidently.

Shannon's nose wrinkled with scepticism. 'Can I take that as gospel?' she quizzed half humorously.

'Okay, I get your meaning—I gather he's still ropeable,' he chuckled. 'Well, why don't you put him back on and I'll square off with him now—tell him it was all my idea and you didn't know anything about it until it was too late,' he proposed generously.

'No, that wouldn't be fair,' she protested, aware the fault had been as much hers as Guy's. 'Besides, I don't really think the present would be an opportune time for...' another look over her shoulder had her encountering a bleak gaze and she swung back again immediately, '... for such things.'

Guy's voice was philosophic as he acceded, 'I guess you know the situation best, so if you want it that way, we'll leave it for the moment.'

'Thanks for the offer though, Guy, and for the call. You don't know how much it's meant to me even though we couldn't say all we wanted to.' And to hell with the construction Mark might choose to put upon those words! At the moment she would have been pleased to talk to the devil himself if he had known of her escapade and didn't condemn her so mercilessly for it.

'My pleasure, love,' Guy discounted her thanks good-naturedly. 'I'm only sorry it didn't work out for you quite the way we planned. Maybe we'll have better luck next time, eh?'

Shannon cut short his laughter with a shudder. 'Don't even think of such a thing! I couldn't bear to go through all this again!' she exclaimed vehemently. And especially not with someone who attracted her as much as Mark did, she added silently.

'Okay, okay, I get the message—once was enough,' he accepted her resolution with merriment evident in his tone, and she blessed his unfailing good spirits which enabled him to see the lighter side of any problem. 'Anyway, I guess I'd better be loving and leaving you for the present, Shannon,' he continued in the same easy way. 'I'll see you at the local festivities ... right?'

'I'll look forward to it,' she smiled. 'It will be good to see you again.'

'Same here, love. Be seeing you.'

As Shannon replaced the receiver in its cradle Mark pushed back his chair and, levering himself to his feet, strode purposefully over to the filing cabinet. She stared doubtfully at his overpowering figure, uncertain whether she should say something or surreptitiously leave the room while she had the chance, but the initiative was taken from her when Mark slapped a file on to the top of the cabinet, pushed in a drawer, and turned to face her. With the elbow of one arm leaning on the fitting, his hand supporting a tenacious jaw while its opposite member rested casually against a supple hip, amber-flecked eyes ranged over her sardonically.

'Found out in more lies, blue eyes?' His voice curled about her forebodingly.

Shannon met his glance warily. 'More lies? I don't follow you,' she frowned.

'No?' Dark brows lifted fractionally. 'Not even when Guy asks to speak to his "best girl",' with a cutting inflection, 'you openly sigh with pleasure at the thought of his coming here and tell him, most impressively, that he couldn't know how much his call meant to you?'

A touch of rebellion settled about her lips. So that remark she made had stirred his suspicions, as she had guessed it might. As for the other, her gasp had been brought about by horror—certainly not pleasure as he was suggesting—and Guy's description of her status in his life—well, that was just Guy and he meant nothing by it. But if Mark was determined to think otherwise, and it seemed that no matter what she said to the contrary he didn't intend to change his opinion, then she would see that she gave him good cause to confirm his misbeliefs.

'All right then, if you must have all the sordid details,' she acquiesced flippantly. 'Yes, I will be pleased to see Guy again,' which wasn't a lie. 'I've been brokenhearted ever since I left him,' which was, 'and I cry myself to sleep every night just thinking about him,' added for good measure.

'But in order to take your mind off him you're not averse to indulging in a little double-dealing on the side?'

Shannon's hands clenched tightly at her sides. 'And just what's that supposed to mean?' she demanded.

'I should have thought it was obvious,' he jeered. 'Everyone on the station knows how you've got Tony dancing on a string, and don't forget,' his voice lowered derisively, 'I happen to know from personal experience just how free your responses are when you're being kissed.'

'All of which means absolutely nothing!' she defended herself haughtily. Having brought up the subject once more she wasn't going to allow him to get the better of her this time. 'Tony is a friend, that's all! As for the other ... well, you—you took me by surprise. You could hardly blame me for not expecting to be kissed while I was being fired, could you?' she questioned sarcastically.

Slowly Mark straightened and moved steadily towards her, causing Shannon to glance away apprehensively as her clutching fingers found the edge of the desk behind her for support.

'So that was brought about by surprise, was it?' he probed lazily as he came to stand a few disturbing feet in front of her.

'N-naturally.' Annoyed to hear her voice wavering uneasily, Shannon berated herself for sounding so dubious and tried desperately to suppress the feeling of trepidation which she discovered was mounting rapidly.

'And any other time your reaction would be quite different, hmm?'

A hasty swallow and Shannon confirmed, 'Of course it would!' in a stronger tone, but couldn't rid herself of the idea that at some point she had completely lost control of the situation—if she had ever had it—and was now being systematically and determinedly outmanoeuvred.

With this thought in the forefront of her mind she began to inch around the corner of the desk and with a nervous laugh flung up her left arm wildly with the pretence of looking at her watch.

'Oh, heavens, look at the time!' she exclaimed in mock amazement. 'I'd better start preparing lunch or it won't be ready on time,' with quickening backward steps in the direction of the doorway.

Three ground-covering strides had Mark's longer arm slamming the door closed before she had time to grip the handle and, in a continuation of the same movement, she was swung around and held captive against the wooden panels by an arm on either side of her head, hands flat against the door.

Mark's head inclined downwards with a cautionary shake. 'Oh, no, you don't, blue eyes,' he drawled mockingly. 'I haven't finished with you yet.'

Shannon licked agitatedly at her lips. 'But—but ... the lunch,' she protested feebly, refusing to lifte her eyes higher than the middle of a wide chest.

'It can wait,' she heard him order peremptorily, and in an effort to regain some of her lost ground she turned taunting eyes upwards to charge, 'Such autocracy!' in her most disdainful voice.

A warm firm hand smoothed against the soft skin of her neck, the thumb pushing aside the collar of her sweater and moving rhythmically in the hollow of her throat where a pulse beat frantically.

'Such hypocrisy!' he mimicked lazily.

Unbearably conscious of his touch, Shannon could feel her knees weakening and she moved restively within the imprisoning arms. 'Hypocrisy?' she repeated huskily, 'I don't know what you mean,' trying hard to fight the lethargy that was stealing over her in a room which seemed to have suddenly become suffocatingly close.

'Meaning that for all your declarations of yearning, you wouldn't, for one moment, think twice about cheating on Guy.'

Why should she? Cheating didn't come into it because there was nothing but friendship between them! But after her earlier protestations, which had been tantamount to an avowed undying love, she could hardly tell Mark how wrong he was.

Instead she denied his allegation with a negative movement of her head and a contradicting, 'You have no proof of that,' which earned a sceptical, 'You think not?' in reply from lips which were only a hair's breadth from her own.

If Shannon had felt her defences were being eroded

before, it was nothing to how she felt now! The warmth of Mark's breath against her mouth was having a cataclysmic effect upon her already raw emotions and two fearful hands pushing against a rugged torso were totally ineffectual in preventing the physical encounter which set her pulses hammering turbulently and dictated that she entreat, 'Mark ... please let me go,' in a humiliating appeal for quarter.

No sooner had she voiced her plea than Mark's shapely mouth closed relentlessly over her own, effectively silencing any further deprecations she might have made, and precipitating her into a world of smouldering desire wherein tantalisingly persuasive lips and the seductive pressure of a hard masculine body had her own lips parting invitingly beneath his, and her slim fingers tangling in the dark curly hair at the back of his head. The hands that had been imprisoning her now slid caressingly down her spine, straining her closer and making her disturbingly aware of her own flagrant ardour until, with a swiftly reversed action, Mark put her away from him stiffly.

'See what I mean?' he queried evenly, though there was a dangerously taut look about the edges of his mouth. 'It really takes very little inducement for you to show your true colours as a two-timing, insincere little liar, doesn't it?'

It took some moments for Shannon to gain some sort of control over her rioting emotions, but when she did it was to stare at him incredulously, her eyes wide and shocked. Was that really all it had meant to him? A cynically enacted experiment to prove a point? She found the idea unbelievable, but a searching look at Mark's harshly set features gave her no reason to think otherwise and she could feel her shoulders beginning to slump dejectedly.

Whether it was brought about by compunction for his pitiless remarks—which idea Shannon immediately discarded—or for some other incomprehensible reason, Mark made a tentative motion with one of his hands towards her, but she stepped quickly out of reach, holding herself rigid and gritting her teeth in an attempt to look unconcerned. She was damned if she'd have him think that those few passionate minutes had meant any more to her than they had to himself.

Determinedly nonchalant, she raised midnight blue eyes to deride, 'And I just *love* you too, *darling*!' with every ounce of mockery she could bring to bear.

This time Mark's advance was definite and without warning. An inescapable hand had gripped Shannon's wrist and dragged her back into his arms before she fully realised what was happening—or could protest—then sank inexorably among her unruly curls. There was nothing persuasive about his mouth when it met hers for the second time either! It was ruthlessly exacting and although Shannon sought valiantly to resist its subjugation, eventually her own senses betrayed her, softening her lips beneath the compelling impact and moulding her body with an alluring pliancy to his hard form as she returned his caresses without restraint.

When Mark finally released her she was pleased to note that his breathing was as deep and heavy as her own and that the hands he hooked into the belt about his lithe waist appeared slightly unsteady.

Not so his voice, however, for he immediately inclined his head to caution with a sardonic accent, 'I wouldn't advise you to use that expression to me again, blue eyes ... not unless you want more of the same, that is.'

Shannon drew air into her lungs angrily. 'Oh, don't worry, I didn't mean it literally!' she scoffed. 'I usually try and keep "darling" reserved for Guy,' she exaggerated with a face-saving facetiousness.

'Then it's a pity you don't keep your amatory instincts reserved for him as well! Or doesn't that fit in with your coquettish little schemes?' he rasped back contemptuously.

The derisive descriptions stabbed acutely and just for a second Shannon couldn't prevent the look of reproach in her eyes, but promptly replaced the expression with one of indifference and a carefully executed shrug.

'Maybe ... maybe not.' She paused and a diligently assumed audacity curved one corner of her mouth. 'And maybe I was only ... practising,' she mocked.

Expecting a savage denigration for her remark, she waited warily in suspense, but when Mark finally broke the disconcerting silence, to her complete amazement, it was with a look and tone that was as mocking as her own had been.

'In which case, I wouldn't suggest you continue the exercise quite so fervently in the future, or you could easily find yourself with a degree of education you're not anticipating,' he advised in a drawl.

There was no mistaking his meaning and Shannon dropped her eyes hastily to avoid the awareness in his, her cheeks colouring warmly and her hands brushing at imaginary pieces of fluff on her sweater. It was all very well mouthing the appropriately insouciant words but, unfortunately, there was no way she could persuade her inherent emotions to automatically follow suit, and consequently her phrases were, as often as not, frustratingly at odds with her reactions.

Now all she had time to murmur was a guarded, 'Yes, well, I ...' before she was interrupted by an extremely exasperated, 'Hell! I'm beginning to understand why Guy was willing to go to such lengths to send you up here!' as a hand raked through dark hair forcefully. 'He probably thought it was preferable to losing his sanity altogether, and I can imagine he needed the respite because you, my fickle little cat, would be more than enough to send him out of his mind!'

Shannon didn't have to pretend to be indignant—it came of its own volition. 'You're so complimentary!' she disparaged resentfully. 'But for your information, Guy didn't send me up here, he just made it possible!'

'With enthusiastic alacrity, I don't doubt,' retorted Mark caustically.

'No!'

'You surprise me,' with a dissident eyebrow quirking upwards.

Shannon's heart sank dejectedly. What was the use? Clearly Mark wasn't ever going to change his mind with regard to what he thought of her, and especially not now that she had recklessly verified his assumption that she and Guy were more than mere friends.

With a defeated movement of her hands she lowered suspiciously bright eyes. 'If that's all, I think I'll get the lunch now,' she murmured heavily, grasping the door handle in readiness.

For a moment it looked as if Mark had something further to say, but then he gave a dismissive shrug, took the file from the cabinet and paced lithely back to his chair.

'Yes, that might be best,' he concurred, coolly impersonal.

In the kitchen Shannon began taking utensils from the appropriate cupboards mechanically, her mind filled with thoughts far less mundane than the preparation of food. It hadn't needed very much soul-searching to discover that the reason Mark could so easily inflict pain was due to the fact that she had fallen in love with him, but that revelation certainly hadn't helped either when she dismally took into account how close he and Hilary were to being married. This was promptly followed by an indignant exclamation. Why hadn't she thought of that before? While he had been righteously censuring with his 'two-timing' and 'insincere' remarks, if she had been thinking more lucidly at the time she could have thrown the very same descriptions back at him. What gave him the right to reprove her when he was guilty of the very same offence? No, worse, because she and Guy were only friends, whereas he was reputed to be as good as engaged to Hilary Donovan! As far as she could see, Mark Seymour lived by double standards—strict values for others, but conveniently lax ones for himself!

All the same, not even this scornful recrimination could quite succeed in lifting her downcast spirits, and the tears that stung her eyelids and were dashed from soft cheeks with the back of an irritable hand weren't entirely due to the onion she was attacking so vigorously on the chopping board.

CHAPTER NINE

THE tightening grip of winter descended upon the table-lands over the following weeks, bringing with it the crisp crunch of silver frosts underfoot in the early morning and, much to Shannon's delight because she had never witnessed it before, a fall of dazzling snow late one grey and sombre afternoon. All too soon, though, it lost its radiant attraction as it became churned in with the mud and shortly after-wards the winds resumed their mournful cries through the paddocks and around the corners of the homestead.

As good as his word, Mark took Shannon with him to the next meeting of the Centenary Committee where, as he had prophesied, an extra volunteer was greeted eagerly, as was her rather tentatively proposed suggestion—after it had been decided that everyone should be invited to attend wearing the dress of the appropriate period—that the food to be served should also conform to that fare eaten by the original settlers.

'What a good idea,' Lyla Unsworth, the secretary of the committee, seconded the idea immediately. 'Others may have dressed the part for their centenaries, but I can't remember hearing of any schools that have provided the relevant type of food as well.'

Mark gave Shannon a sideways glance from where he perched on the corner of one of the desks—primary school chairs weren't accommodating to someone of his long leg-ged-proportions.

'Just mutton and damper?' he bent to query her desire to provide unleavened bread in mock disbelief.

'You forgot the black billy tea,' she reminded him with a challenging smile. 'And I wasn't advocating that we restrict ourselves to the bare basics, even though that was the staple diet for many of the pioneers. There are lots of other dishes they made which would be suitable. Although, while we're on the subject of the basics, an animal of some kind would need to be spit-roasted, wouldn't it?' she probed in round-eyed innocence.

He gave her a wry look. 'Beef or lamb?'

Taking courage from the talk around her and Mark's own relaxed mood, Shannon wrinkled her nose disarmingly and ventured, 'Both, actually. By the sound of it there should be well over a couple of hundred people present, and it always seems as if people's appetites double on occasions like these.'

'I'm beginning to think I've been had!' Mark laughed tolerantly, making her heart thud noisily against her ribs at the sound of it. 'Okay, blue eyes, just tell Trevor what you want and when, and he'll kill and dress them for you.'

'And we can donate a pig to make sure that all tastes are catered for,' said Lyla, including her husband, Kevin, with a waving hand, on overhearing their conversation. 'Did you have any particular ideas in mind what we could serve, Shannon?' she asked next.

'Well, I suppose you would have to include the faithful old damper,' with a provoking glance from beneath thickly fringed lashes at Mark. 'And, by rights, it should be cooked in the hot embers of an open fire, or in an old iron camp oven. Or it can be served in a multitude of different ways; as Johnny Cakes—smaller, individual portions . . .'

'Or as sinkers—which is the damper dough boiled and eaten with lashings of golden syrup,' laughed Eve Gilbert, whose husband was another member of the committee. 'I can remember devouring those with great delight when we used to visit our grandmother as kids.'

'Or in the form of doughboys—which has suet added to it and is then boiled like yours, Eve, and eaten with dark molasses—or blackstrap, as our grandparents used to call it,' added Lyla with a grin.

'Or as puftaloons—when it's fried in fat,' put in another of the ladies present, but whose name Shannon couldn't remember.

Now that the idea was really in motion, suggestions began coming in from all sides of the room.

'Fruit pies, crisp potato cakes, soda bread . . .'

'Seed cake, plum cakes, sponges . . .'

'Pumpkin pie, gramma pie, and meringue cakes . . .'

'Custards, jellies—with real fruit, of course, none of your packet stuff this time—fruit creams and blancmanges.'

'Marzipan balls, syllabubs, flummeries and busters,' Shannon added some of her own known recipes.

'Busters?' echoed Eve with a smile and a frown. 'That's a new one on me—what were they?'

'Like a kind of scone, only they have cheese and cayenne pepper in them,' Shannon explained with an answering smile.

Once the suggestions for food had been talked out the discussion turned to the advertisements that would need to be inserted in the newspapers, and it was decided that all the State capitals would need to be covered, as well as the rural areas, if all former pupils and residents were to be notified of the coming celebrations. Lyla made some appropriate notes, for, as she was secretary, it would fall to her to see that the right papers were contacted, and then it was time for those articles of interest already unearthed to be handed over to Colin Pritchard, the teacher who would keep them safe at the school until they went on display.

Some of the items—such as century-old shearing tally books, wages books and diaries—generated a great deal of interest. Others, like the ancient and tattered School Punishment Book, brought sounds of commiseration for the boy of four and a half who was caned for whistling in school; and smiles at the thought of their own escapes from punishment for doing the same as the boy of nine who was also meted out the same penance for throwing seeds at the other pupils while the teacher was absent from the room.

Chuckles greeted some of the resurrected photographs, especially those depicting early schooldays as mothers, fathers and even grandparents were recognised among the stiffly posed students. Still others showed bygone school fetes, tennis matches—the women in long heavy skirts and incongruously modish hats, groups of children riding to school—as often as not with two or more riding the one horse, split-log and shingle cottages—their owners standing uneasily for the photographer on the verandahs; and stalwart-looking men with axes and mattocks in hand as they hewed out empires for themselves in a raw and uncompromising land.

It was close to midnight before supper was concluded and everyone had been assigned an area to cover in their search for relics and curios over the ensuing weeks, and in the warm confines of the car on their way home Shannon turned her head warily when Mark began to speak.

'Don't you think you could be taking on too much with all the help you offered tonight?' he questioned.

'I don't think so,' she contradicted swiftly. 'After all, I won't be doing more than any other woman who was there tonight.'

'But they're locals.'

And I'm not! I'm an outsider who's only here under

sufferance, thought Shannon miserably, drawing on her cigarette and knocking the ash from its tip shakily as she murmured a subdued, 'Oh, I see.'

Mark's scrutiny was swift, but encompassing, before he turned his eyes back to the road glistening before them in the glow of the headlights.

'I doubt it,' he drawled lazily. 'But I would be interested to hear just what it is you think you see.'

'I doubt it!' The bitterly mimicking words earned a smothered exclamation and a taut:

'And what's that supposed to imply?'

With the congenial mood of the evening shattering around her, Shannon shrugged deeper into her jacket moodily. 'Does it matter? You made your point.'

'Thanks for letting me know—I wasn't aware I had one to make!'

'Oh, don't give me that,' Shannon rounded on him resentfully. 'You made it perfectly plain you consider I'm intruding where I'm not wanted.'

A hand snaked out to grasp the nape of her neck and give her head anything but a gentle shake before returning to the wheel.

'You idiotic little...' He broke off angrily. 'Then why the hell would I have bothered to invite you to the meeting in the first place?'

Shannon shook her head and stubbed out her cigarette roughly. 'How should I know?' she returned acidly, reluctant to admit she might have misjudged him, but relieved to hear the grid rattle beneath the tyres as they turned on to the property and know that freedom was close at hand.

As soon as the vehicle had drawn into the garage, Shannon released her seatbelt and made a hasty grab for the door handle, but a detaining hand around her upper arm precluded any exit.

'Sit tight, blue eyes!' she was ordered in a drawling intonation. 'We still have things to discuss.'

'Such as?'

'Such as—how you would suddenly get such a dimwitted idea that your help wasn't wanted?'

Shannon's resentment rose at his disparaging description and she pulled free of his restraining hand peevishly to enquire, 'Does it matter?' with unaccustomed rancour.

'Yes, damn you, it does!' Mark swept an exasperated hand around the back of his neck before commanding in the same explosive tones, 'So, for heaven's sake, stop feeling sorry for yourself and get whatever's bothering you off your chest and be done with it!'

The knowledge that she might have been displaying a trait she didn't normally indulge had Shannon glaring at him rebelliously, her denial over-vehement.

'I was not feeling sorry for myself!' she snapped. 'But—but what did you expect me to think when you so kindly pointed out that everyone else working for the committee was a local?' in justification.

'Perhaps I expected you to do just that—think, not jump to conclusions!' he informed her with a kind of sardonic patience. 'Lyla and Eve and the rest of the women down there tonight know what they're letting themselves in for. When you go visiting those properties you have on your list, it won't be ten-minute calls you'll be making—in most cases you'll be expected to stay for a meal as well—and I don't know how many hours you have in your day, blue eyes, but everyone else only has twenty-four!'

'If the others can do it, so can I!' she retorted confidently.

'They also happen to have housekeepers to keep things running in their absence.'

This smoothly supplied information halted Shannon abruptly, but only until she had collected her thoughts and then she turned on him sarcastically.

'So that's what's bothering you!' Her eyes widened

scornfully. 'You're just worried that I'll let the house-keeping slide. You think...'

'Don't be so damned ridiculous!' he interrupted incisively, jaw outthrust. 'As unbelievable as it may seem, my concern was for *you*, not the homestead! There is a limit to how much one person can do, you know.'

There was a ring of truth to his peremptory statement she couldn't dispute. Not that she really wanted to, for if she was honest with herself, she found the idea of his solicitude rather warming, even though she was well aware it was nothing more than that of an employer for an employee.

'Yes, well...' She moved uncomfortably in her seat and sighed. 'I'm sorry, Mark, I didn't know that was what you meant.' A shaky smile and she couldn't help chiding, 'But then I am more accustomed to moralising than anxiety from you, aren't I?'

A disturbingly pleasurable glow crept over her at the sound of Mark's surprisingly indulgent laughter which was by no means diminished when his arm stretched along the back of the seat and one finger tormentingly twined among her soft curls.

'Is that a reprimand, or a request for closer attention?' he murmured provocatively.

Shannon bit at her lip and swallowed hard. 'N-neither,' she protested breathlessly. 'I was merely stating a fact, that's all.'

'But a disagreeable one, hmm?'

Now that his fingers were slipping lower to caress the side of her neck it was all the more difficult for Shannon to think straight, and she knew that if she passively sat there any longer it would be impossible not to reveal her true feelings, so she shrugged out from under his touch, an unsteady hand groping for the door catch, and managed to conjure up a sufficiently jaunty curve to her lips.

'I'll survive,' she parried flippantly.

'I'm sure you will,' Mark conceded evenly. 'Your kind usually does.'

Shannon pushed open the door and swung her legs wrathfully to the ground. 'At least that's comforting to know!' she flung back at him over one shoulder. 'After all, we are advised to use our natural abilities to their best advantage, aren't we? And I would hate to think I was allowing any of mine to go unfulfilled!' slamming the door closed stormily behind her and running frantically for the house, her thoughts seething.

Inside her room she hurriedly threw off her coat and fumbled a cigarette from the packet in her bag. Lighting it, she paced restlessly to and fro across the room, then, just as impulsively, she turned and ground it out again in the ashtray.

It wasn't only Mark's opinion of her that was causing such unease, there was her own vulnerability in his presence to consider as well. For how long could she use self malignment as a form of protection? It was all very well using Guy as a cover, but what when he actually arrived? It wouldn't take long for someone as discerning as Mark to realise there were no strong emotional ties between them, and then it would only be a short step to uncovering her real secret.

She wrapped her arms about her midriff and closed her eyes momentarily. Apart from keeping out of Mark's way as much as possible, she really had very little choice. Let him think she was a two-timer and all the rest he had called her—she wouldn't be disabusing him of the idea, if that was the only way to keep the truth to herself. In the meantime, she would learn as much as she could from Tony, because she knew only too well that once Mark and Hilary became engaged—a stabbing pain caught at her heart at the thought—then she would be forced to seek a position elsewhere. Loving him as she did, there was no way in the world she would be able to continue working on Tuesday and watch his love being given to someone else. She just wasn't that self-destructive!

Much to Shannon's surprise Nola Seymour asked to accompany her on some of her forays for exhibits, which requests she promptly accepted as she was never quite certain she was on the right route, as some of the properties were a long way from the beaten track, and still being a little unsure of her own driving capabilities she felt more secure when someone was with her.

Although the older woman usually gave the impression of being slightly muddle-headed when it came to anything besides her beloved art, during their days together Shannon found that this was extremely misleading for, having been born and raised in the district, Nola knew a great deal of its history and alleviated the monotony of the many miles they covered with interesting narrations and amusing reminiscences, while being extremely perceptive as to the articles likely to generate the most interest and to suit the display most effectively. Which really shouldn't have astonished her so greatly, Shannon mused thoughtfully, for to be as good an artist as Nola Seymour undoubtedly was, one needed more than just a pair of eyes and a dexterous hand—there had to be an alert and discriminating intelligence as well.

Of course Pete and Tony didn't always agree with their choice and on many occasions there were bantering exchanges when collections were unveiled in the back of the ute, but if Mark agreed with them he kept his comments to himself, seemingly as desirous as Shannon of keeping a tempering distance between them.

As the motion had been unanimously accepted at the meeting, a trip into Narrawa with Betty Lovett provided them with the material and patterns for their nineteenth-century gowns, and their evenings became filled with dressmaking as the weeks wore on.

Even Hilary joined them one night instead of spending the time with Mark after she and her father had dined at Tuesday—which action had Shannon frowning in speculation as to the reason until she remembered that Mark had been absent from the homestead most nights that week, and reasoned that Hilary no doubt felt she could spare his company for a few hours. And jealous though she might have been—a reluctant but truthful confession—Shannon couldn't help but like the other girl. Outgoing and friendly, she had a warm and understanding nature which was impossible to dislike.

Once the winds of winter had blown themselves out, the days started to lengthen again and although the air was still brisk and frosty in the early light of morning, by midday the sun was once again in command and the burgeoning trees began to show their appreciation with unfurling leaves and sprouting blossoms.

The men were now busy on the run mustering lambs for drenching prior to weaning, and preparing the ewes for the coming spring drop, but every so often Tony managed to find time—when Mark was safely out of the way, of course—to continue Shannon's riding lessons, although on some occasions she had to forgo the opportunity because she hadn't the time herself. Nevertheless, she was pleased with the progress she was making and most evenings saw her down at the bails helping with the milking.

The last few weeks prior to the Centenary had been active ones for Shannon too, as she was finding that her association with Tuesday—or more particularly, with Mark —put her in the forefront of the action, and an amazingly large part of her days seemed to be taken up with either receiving, or making, telephone calls on behalf of the committee, and so, with only five more days to go, when she heard the sound of a car pulling up in front of the homestead she walked down the hall and out on to the verandah expecting another enquiry concerning the school.

Her ready smile of welcome turned to one of delight as she saw Guy's fair head emerging from the vehicle, but it faded to a lip-chewing consternation when her glance crossed with Mark's stony gaze from the driver's side. Obviously he had known of the Crawfords' pending arrival—both Guy's father, and a small white-haired woman she presumed was his mother, were alighting now—and just as obviously he had deliberately kept it a secret—from her, anyway. Now she moved slowly towards the steps, rubbing the palms of her hands nervously down the sides of her jeans.

Guy's approach had no such reservations, however, for he strode up the steps with a wide grin and, catching Shannon completely off guard, wrapped his arms around her to exuberantly sweep her off her feet before gaily planting a resounding kiss on her unexpectant mouth. As he lowered her back to the ground his head angled downwards conspiratorially.

'I see you're still in one piece,' he whispered with a laugh. 'After that phone call I was beginning to have my doubts as to whether I did the right thing in arranging for you to come up here.' He looked down at her thoughtfully, if a little perplexedly. 'Mark really took it that hard, did he?'

When she had regained some of her composure after his totally unanticipated greeting, Shannon's arched brows peaked so expressively in answer that her wry, 'You could say that!' really wasn't necessary.

'Never mind, love,' Guy smiled, and draped a consoling arm over her shoulders. 'Come and meet the other half of my parents. She's heard quite a lot about you, one way and another. First from me, at home, and now Mark on the way here from the station.'

For a moment Shannon hung back against his arm, dismay covering her face. 'He hasn't told him, has he?' she gasped, horrified.

An uncomprehending frown. 'Told who what?'

'Mark told your father about us, of course!'

'Oh, that!' Guy shook his head negligently. 'Not while we were in the car, he didn't,' he gave her reason to sigh with relief. 'We were mainly talking about the celebrations and Mark was telling us what a help you'd been to the committee.'

Shannon overcame her moment's wonderment that Mark could have managed to find something pleasant to say about her for a change to surmise caustically, 'Saving the best news for last, I suppose.'

If Guy was in agreement with her assumption he wasn't given a chance to say so, as his parents and Mark had now reached the verandah steps and the next few minutes were occupied with Shannon being introduced to Audrey Crawford and renewing her acquaintance with Guy's father.

'From what Mark has been saying, you appear to have settled in here well, Shannon. Not too much of a change after Atyimba, I hope,' Mr Crawford smiled kindly down at her.

'Um—er ...' Shannon's fleeting glance intercepted a cynical twist to Mark's lips and she turned back quickly to the man in front of her. 'No, not really, thank you, Mr Crawford,' she responded more surely. As she had never actually been there, how could she notice the difference?

'Oh, Shannon's very adaptable,' Mark put in silkily. 'She has an inimitable way of making do with what's available.'

Which remark had Shannon laughing lightly in return, 'I do my best, boss, I do my my best,' even though her temper threatened to explode inside her and her eyes blazed at him furiously.

'That's good, then,' Harold Crawford applauded warmly, obviously unaware of the mounting tension or the sardonic undercurrents. 'It seems as if I might have found the right jillaroo for you at last, eh, Mark?'

Her slim figure stiff with apprehension, Shannon waited

expectantly for Mark's denunciation, but his drawled, 'You may be right, Harry,' threw her so completely off balance that she was left staring at him in astonishment until she received a mockingly lifted brow in return and she turned her head away again in confusion.

She couldn't believe that Mark didn't eventually intend to tell Guy's father of her deception and she could only presume that it was for some obscure reason of his own that he hadn't done so when presented with such an opportune moment. Doubtless he was only holding his silence until he tired of keeping her on tenterhooks and would bring his cat-and-mouse game to an ignominious end at his own pleasure.

When he ushered Mr and Mrs Crawford into the home-stead, Shannon found she was bringing up the rear with Guy, but, standing to one side, Mark indicated that the younger man should precede him and put a detaining hand around Shannon's wrist.

'I think Audrey and Harry will be best suited in the double bedroom next to Nola,' he said quietly, his head low so that the others didn't overhear. 'The room next to yours will do for Guy, but it would be as well to remember, blue eyes, that even though he may be your one and only *true love*,' with such chaffing sarcasm that it was all she could do not to hit out at him with one of her doubling fists, 'I won't tolerate having this household disturbed by Guy's, or your, nightly wanderings!'

Outrage had Shannon gasping and firing back before she had really made up her mind what to say. 'Then it might have been more considerate if you'd thought of that earlier and installed a connecting door between the two, mightn't it?' she retorted tartly, and promptly fled fearfully after the others without giving Mark a chance to exchange the omin-ous look descending on to his face for what she knew would be equally devastating words ... or worse!

Shannon was well aware that it was only the fact there were

guests in the house that had prevented her being called to account, and in no uncertain terms, for her most recent rash and impetuous outburst to Mark, but she hadn't realised that their cool avoidance of each other had been quite so noticeable until the afternoon that Guy came into the kitchen while she was preparing some of the food which was to be stored in the freezer until the weekend.

Hooking a stool towards himself, he sat with his arms resting on the breakfast bar and a curious expression in his blue eyes.

'I was talking to Mark this morning,' he began slowly. 'Or perhaps I should say, Mark was talking to me,' ruefully, but watching Shannon closely, although apart from a slight hesitation in her rolling of the pastry on the floured board there was no sign that she had heard anything untoward. 'Somewhere along the line he seems to have gained the impression that we're ... how shall I put it ...?'

Shannon sighed and looked up. 'More than friends?' she finished for him wryly.

'Uh-huh,' he grinned, reaching for a handful of sultanas from an opened packet on the bench.

'Do you mind?'

He chewed thoughtfully, swallowed, and shook his head. 'I wouldn't have, if I'd known about it beforehand. As it turned out, I felt rather like a canoeist cut loose without a paddle,' he owned with an engaging smile.

'I'm sorry,' she apologised contritely. 'But you didn't tell him the truth?' anxiously.

Guy laughed goodnaturedly. 'No, but I would like to know how it came about. Was it your idea, or his?'

'Mark's originally. When he discovered I hadn't any experience he accurately guessed that you'd helped me and arbitrarily decided that that must have been the reason—a deduction he's simply refused to alter even when I refuted it. And now ...' she lifted her shoulders helplessly.

'And now ...?' he repeated incorrigibly. 'As a form of

protection ... or to make him jealous?'

'Certainly not the latter!' she protested indignantly, her face colouring at the idea.

'But you are hooked on him, though, aren't you, love?'

Was there any use in denying it? And if she had to confess to somebody, she would rather it was Guy, so with a wan, self-mocking smile she nodded her acknowledgment heavily.

Guy bit through more sultanas. 'So where's the problem? He's still single, isn't he?'

Uncaring of the flour, Shannon's hands thumped on to her hips. 'Where's the problem, he asks! Are you serious?' she mocked incredulously. 'Oh, apart from the fact that he considers I'm deceitful, disloyal and dishonest—on top of which he happens to be on the point of becoming engaged—there isn't one that I can think of!' she retorted with a meaningful flourish of her hands.

'You have got yourself in a mess, haven't you?' he grinned ruefully, and had Shannon pulling a grimacing face at him in retaliation. 'Who's the other girl in this triangle?'

When he heard Hilary Donovan's name his mouth turned down judicially and his gaze became sympathetic. 'That's tough,' he conceded. 'Other than acting as a bulwark, is there anything else I can do to help? Another job perhaps?' he tried to bring some lightheartedness into the situation.

'I might even take you up on that,' she responded to his encouragement with a smile. 'Only next time I'll make sure I start off with everything fair, square and above board, because I certainly don't intend to go through anything like this again.'

'Mmm, knowing Mark as I do, I can imagine he was pretty intimidating when he first found out, but even so, I really didn't exepect him to take it with quite such an unrelenting intolerance.' He scratched at his head wonderingly. 'You have had a lousy time of it, haven't you, love?'

But somehow all that had gone before seemed to pale

into insignificance for Shannon on Friday morning. She had
been answering yet another phone call requesting the com-
mencement time for the celebrations on the morrow when
she heard Mark's voice in the hallway and, replacing the
receiver, she turned to see him escorting a middle-aged
woman with round rosy cheeks and a wide smiling mouth
into the room.

'Shannon, I'd like you to meet Beryl Dobson ...
Trevor's mother,' he added by way of explanation.

'I'm pleased to meet you, Mrs Dobson,' Shannon shook
the older woman's hand warmly, a natural smile disclosing
sparkling white teeth. 'Have you come to stay for the
Centenary?'

'For longer than that, I hope,' she returned with a laughing sideways look at Mark.

'Beryl has been our housekeeper for the last fifteen years.
You remember, I told you she'd moved south to look after
her sister? Well, apparently now that her niece has returned
from overseas and will be caring for her mother, Beryl of
course had no reason to stay any longer.'

Mark's casually inparted information reverberated about
Shannon's ears deafeningly and the smile on her lips became tightly fixed. She noted that he had said 'has been'
and not 'was' their housekeeper. That tense made all the
difference! Now she knew why he hadn't been in a hurry to
advertise for a permanent housekeeper! Why he had always
made it plain he only considered *her* temporary! Oh, God,
did he really despise her so much that he couldn't have
found some less callous way of letting her know she had
been replaced? Why hadn't anybody else thought to tell her
that Trevor's mother normally held her position? Or perhaps they were under the impression she was already aware
of the fact. As more of the same desolating thoughts spun
wildly in her mind a burning pain of mortification rose
slowly from the pit of her stomach to rest chokingly at the
base of her throat, but she knew she wasn't a good enough

actress to disguise the torment that was dimming her eyes and after one involuntary—and immediately regretted—anguished glance in Mark's direction, she bowed her head in self-preservation.

An outstretched hand hovered tentatively in her line of vision and then disappeared, but when curiosity made her raise her head slightly, it was to find Beryl Dobson peering at her worriedly.

'You've gone quite white, dear. I do hope my sudden return to Tuesday isn't the cause of it,' she said, and looked across at Mark questioningly. 'Perhaps I should have given you more notice of my arrival, Mark? But I had no idea you'd managed to find such a capable substitute and I, obviously mistakenly, believed I would be helping if I returned as soon as possible.'

The brief interlude had at least given Shannon time to recover some of her composure and now she used it for her own protection before Mark had a chance to humble her further.

'Oh, no, Mrs Dobson, it was nothing like that. I expect it was just the fact that I've been rushing this morning,' her lying assurance tumbled out swiftly. It wasn't Trevor's mother's fault that Mark Seymour couldn't wait to be rid of her. 'I-I've known right from the beginning that my employment here would be a case of "here today, gone tomorrow".' She dragged out a shaky laugh and knew that Mark would have preferred that to read 'gone yesterday'. 'Really, I was surprised it lasted this long,' with an increasingly indifferent lift to her chin.

The strained expression eased from Beryl Dobson's face. 'Well, that does make me feel better,' she sighed happily. 'But now, if you'll both excuse me, I think I'll just sort out my things in my room and then I'll be along to give you whatever assistance you need, Shannon. As Mark knows only too well,' with a nostalgic smile, 'I never like to be out of harness for too long!'

Watching while the older woman disappeared through the doorway, Shannon wondered if her feet had taken root, for, as much as she willed them to carry her likewise, her legs remained adamantly weak and it wasn't until Mark crossed to her side and a warm demoralising hand touched her shoulder and he queried, 'Shannon, didn't Chris ...' that the floodgates on her emotions opened wide, allowing all her pent-up hurt and resentment to flow forth.

'*I hate you*, Mark Seymour!' she flung her interruption at him fiercely through gritted teeth, whirling out of his reach, her breath coming in fast and heavy gulps. 'Hate you more than anyone I've ever hated in my life before! Believe me, I shall be just as pleased to leave here as you will be to see me go!' with a defensively challenging look in her eyes. 'When's the next train out of here? Tomorrow morning? Good, I'll be on it!'

With fingers hooked indolently into the belt of his close-fitting denims, Mark appeared quite impervious to her emotionalism as his mouth crooked nonchalantly and he drawled unhelpfully, 'I wasn't planning on sending a vehicle into Narrawa tomorrow.'

'So I'll thumb a lift!'

'I doubt even that will do you much good this weekend. As we're not on the main highway most of the cars that use this road are locally owned, and I think you already know yourself in which direction they'll be travelling in the morning,' he pointed out evenly, aggravatingly sure of himself.

Some of the explosiveness in Shannon's fury began to subside as she recognised the truth of what he was saying, but she wasn't about to meekly acquiesce to his plausible reasoning so she shrugged blithely and suggested, 'Then I'll walk to the highway and catch a lift from there into town. I'll write and advise you where to send my cases once I've found a place to live.'

'As long as you don't expect to receive them.'

'What do you mean ... don't expect to receive them?'

she frowned. Then her face cleared and she taunted, 'Oh, don't panic, I'll send the money for the freight with my letter, if that's what's bothering you.'

She had the heart-stopping suspicion it was only due to the strongest self-control on Mark's part that she wasn't physically made to pay for that insolent insinuation, and she let out her breath thankfully when his voice was only a shade or two cooler than it had been as he relayed, 'They still won't be forwarded,' in the same obstructive fashion.

'And why not?' she demanded.

'Because I shall keep them in lieu of the month's service to which I'm entitled when you quit.'

The full implication of his comment was lost on Shannon as she protested reproachfully, 'But you can't do that!'

Mark flexed his shoulder muscles unconcernedly and she could feel the burning heat of magnetism racing distractingly within her veins at the fascinating smile shaping the firm mouth which lazily proposed, 'Try me.'

Whether the resolution was legal or not Shannon didn't know, but she could be reasonably certain that Mark didn't care—he could always say her luggage had been misplaced, couldn't he?—and the only person likely to be disconcerted by his high-handed action would be herself. She chewed at her lip doubtfully for a few seconds until her eyes began to widen when realisation dawned and she stared at him in disbelief.

'*Quit!*' The word stabbed into the air accusingly. 'I didn't quit ... you *fired* me!' she charged furiously.

'Did I? I wasn't aware of it,' he countered mockingly.

The soft material of her shirt moulded itself to her breasts as she heaved with resentment. 'What else would you call it then when you confront someone with their successor? Reassurance?'

'That would depend on the reason for the replacement, wouldn't you say?'

Shannon swept back the curls from her forehead with a

diffident hand. 'I s-suppose so,' she admitted reluctantly, waiting for him to continue, which he did with calculated goading.

'And as I haven't ... as yet,' oh, yes, he would have to add that little rider, noted Shannon scornfully, 'actually said that you've been discharged, then you can presume that you're still on the payroll, can't you, blue eyes?'

For the moment her curiosity overpowered her indignation and she queried puzzledly, 'Doing what?' with a plaintive bewilderment that had her mouth tightening in disgust when she heard it.

'For the present,' he left her in irritating suspense as he made slowly for the door, 'I think you'll find the Centenary sufficient to keep you well occupied,' he tossed over his shoulder noncommittally before stepping out into the hall and pulling the door closed behind him.

Left staring at the polished panels, Shannon lifted her hands into the air and then slapped them against her legs in a defeated gesture. What was the use in even attempting to flout him? In the space of half an hour he had successfully run her through a gamut of emotions ranging from unqualified shock to outright retreat—not forgetting a sprinkling of hate, sarcasm, attraction and resentment on the way, she reminded herself derisively—but now he had managed to leave her intrigued and totally confused as well!

CHAPTER TEN

IMMEDIATELY she awoke the next morning Shannon flung back the covers on her bed and raced for the window. Raising her eyes skywards, she smiled happily. The weather was holding good and it was going to be another fine day. Already the pale incandescence of the sun had cleared the tree tops and was bathing the dew-speckled pastures with a clear, pearly light, and causing the long morning shadows to shorten, inch by inch, the higher it ascended. After all their efforts it would have been too deflating if the elements had turned against them.

A quick shower and she was soon scrambling into blue denims and a lemon shirt, dragging on a pair of brown leather sandals and heading directly for the kitchen. She was going to have to move fast this morning if she was to be down at the school in time to help add the finishing touches before the first of the visitors began arriving.

On stepping through the doorway she was greeted by Beryl Dobson in the act of taking delivery of the morning milk from her son—who was promptly shooed outside again by his parent when he showed signs of lingering to talk—and recalling to Shannon's mind the fact that Tony would already be at the school taking his turn with the slow roasting of the carcases which had been shipped down the previous afternoon.

'Everything's ready for you, Shannon,' smiled Beryl helpfully, bringing a jug of milk across to the breakfast bar. 'You just have your breakfast and I'll attend to anything that needs doing in the homestead this morning.' She looked about her ruefully. 'Not that you've left me much,' she chuckled. 'You must have been very busy these last few weeks.'

'I must admit there were times when we didn't think we

would get it all completed,' Shannon laughed, pouring milk into her cup ready for the tea Beryl had just brewed, and helping herself to toast and marmalade. 'You have no idea just what an assortment we managed to uncover. Some of them, I'm sure, haven't seen the light of day for over half a century.'

'And I understand you're all dressing like they used to as well?'

'Mmm, although I wish they'd been a little more anxious to show something of themselves. What with those long sleeves, high necklines and voluminous skirts, goodness only knows how they managed to survive in this climate.'

'I've often wondered that myself,' conceded Beryl with a smile. 'And especially since most of their food was made up of heavy, starchy dishes which could hardly have made pleasant eating during an Australian summer either.'

'Well, we shouldn't have that problem today,' Shannon grinned. 'I think there'll be a range of food at the school to please everyone's taste.' She glanced down at her watch and hastily swallowed the last of her breakfast, which was just as quickly followed by the remains of her tea. 'But I'd better get dressed soon or I won't have everything ready to load into the wagon when Pete brings it round.'

'Off you go, then,' Beryl urged. 'Leave all this to me.'

With a grateful, 'Thank you,' Shannon needed no second bidding and was hurrying to her room almost before the other woman had a chance to lightly dismiss her indebtedness.

The hydrangea blue dress with its full waist-diminishing skirt and lacy high-collared bodice clung to Shannon's curving figure becomingly, while the pale straw boater-type hat she had discovered in a crowded boutique in Narrawa—a band of blue lace now surrounding its crown—perched with a jaunty air on the top of her curly head and put the final touch to her old-fashioned creation.

Her smooth skin, appropriately clear of make-up—apart

from a faint but very effective trace of eyeshadow and the palest of rose-coloured lipsticks—was glowing delicately from anticipation as well as exertion when Pete bounded up the verandah steps an hour or so later with his called, 'You ready yet, Shannon?' preceding him into the kitchen.

'Just about,' she replied lightly, her arms loaded with containers and boxes she intended to hand across so that he could take them down to the station wagon, and burst out laughing when he strode into the room and stopped dead at the sight of her, a long low whistle expressing his feelings.

'Hell!' burst from his lips incredulously. 'I always knew you had looks, but you've really outdone yourself today,' he offered in unabashed admiration. 'If you're an example of what they used to look like in those days ... man, oh, man, I'm obviously living in the wrong century,' he grinned.

'Yes, she does look pretty, doesn't she?' Beryl added her own observation with a smile and Shannon, still laughing, made a mock curtsey in return for his extravagant compliments.

Finally he came to the realisation that he hadn't as yet relieved her of her burden and with an apologetic, 'Here, let me take those,' he held out his hands and juggled the canisters more securely against his chest once she had passed them over before heading back to the verandah. 'Are there any more of these to come?' he asked casually without slowing his pace.

Shannon and Beryl exchanged grins. 'A few,' they understated together, picturing the amount still waiting in the pantry.

The packing completed at last, Pete saw Shannon into the passenger seat of the wagon. 'You're not supposed to be feeding all the visitors on your own, you know,' he laughed, and indicated the stacked containers with a nod of his head. 'You're sure you haven't mistakenly got the kitchen sink in there too?'

Eyes wide, Shannon pretended dismay. 'You mean, I

forgot it?' she asked innocently, and made to get out of the car.

'Oh, no, you don't,' he grinned, and prevented her exit with a closed door. 'We're leaving before you get any more ideas,' he declared emphatically after walking around to take his own seat.

A wrinkled nose was all he received in return until a thought suddenly flashed into her mind and she glanced at him enquiringly. 'I've just remembered something—I haven't seen Guy yet this morning. Isn't he supposed to be coming with us?'

'He was,' Pete agreed, 'but Mark altered the arrangements late last night and took Guy with him when he went earlier. His parents, my mother, and Beryl, will all be coming down together later,' he went on informatively, turning the vehicle on to the bitumen.

'Apart from Beryl, I haven't even seen anyone else today.'

'Probably trying to keep out of the way so that we could get there on time,' he suggested logically. 'There's no need for them to rush.'

'Mmm, I guess not.'

The miles to Seymour Vale were quickly covered, but once they had arrived it took Shannon some moments before she could distinguish some form of order amidst the chaotic activity that was taking place. There seemed to be people rushing in all directions carrying one thing or another and, after unloading the car for her, Pete excused himself with a casual salute and a wry, 'I guess I'd better find Mark. I expect he'll have something arranged for me to do.'

She watched him striding past the oak trees to where a group of men were clustered around the open fire pit, a smile on her face. She expected Mark would have something for him to do too! He didn't know it yet, but there were stalls still to be erected, banners to be strung between the trees, as well as pony rides and hayrides to be arranged.

The next hour and a half passed by swiftly, but by the time the first of the visitors began arriving and reunions were being made with long-forgotten school friends, the stalls for serving the food and refreshments had all been completed and stocked, while the records and exhibits had been arranged either inside the school, or, in the case of the old farming implements, in one corner of the grounds. The camp ovens for cooking the dampers were lined up in readiness on the verandah and the aroma from the sizzling meats on the spits was making many a nose twitch appreciatively.

'I don't know about you, but I could do with something to drink,' said Eve Gilbert, pulling at the neck of her own close-fitting, leg-of-mutton-sleeved blouse, when she and Shannon had pinned the last of the photographs to the classroom wall. 'How does a cool lemon squash sound?' she smiled.

'Like a lifesaver at the moment,' laughed Shannon, leading the way down the steps and over the grass to the stall where Lyla was serving drinks. 'I'm beginning to wonder if I did the right thing in suggesting we wear period clothes.'

'No, that was a good idea,' Eve refused to agree to such a suggestion. 'My three daughters—who are around here somewhere,' she shaded her eyes with a hand to peer experimentally into the increasing crowd, but gave it up in the end with a light-hearted shrug, 'had a great time choosing designs for us all. They made their frocks in their sewing classes at high school in town. I'll have to introduce them to you, or at least, I will if I can find them,' she laughed.

'Find what?' asked Lyla when they came to a halt in front of her stall. 'Don't tell me we've lost something already.'

Eve shook her head reassuringly. 'Only some of my tribe,' she explained. 'Shannon hasn't met them yet.'

Lyla nodded comprehendingly. 'I'm glad that's all it

was, because I don't think I could stand any more panic at the moment. My place was like a madhouse with the kids this morning, and I forgot the camp oven which we had to go back for. Then, as we came past, Kevin noticed that one of the bulls had broken through his fence, so we had to wait until he'd taken him across to the west paddock, and while all this was happening young Patrick wanted to see if there were any tadpoles in the creek yet, and of course I don't need to tell you what happened next, so back to the house we went again so he could change into some dry clothes. I tell you, I can hardly believe it's still only nine-thirty. I feel as if I've done a full day's work already,' she laughed ruefully.

'Then you'd better share a drink with us,' suggested Eve, her eyes twinkling. 'How about pouring three lemon squashes for three squashed—should I continue the pun and say . . . lemons?' which had all three of them laughing.

'I'm surprised at you, Eve,' a lazy voice admonished from behind Shannon. 'Suggesting that three of our most attractive womenfolk should be classified in such a category!'

There was no need for Shannon to look to discover who the speaker was, she would know that voice anywhere—but look she did—she just couldn't help herself, the compulsion was too strong to resist. It was the first time she had seen Mark that morning, and in cream belted moleskins, open-necked tan and white plaid check shirt, the sleeves rolled up past the elbows to display brown muscular forearms, and an ever-faithful bush hat seated squarely on his dark head, he looked so provokingly and dangerously male that she immediately felt her heart begin its customary pounding and her legs grow unsteady.

A condition which didn't improve in the slightest when he casually leant one of those strong arms proprietorially across her shoulders, and even though she kept telling herself that she was a fool to let him have such an effect on her when she was all too aware that he was about to become engaged to another girl—and one whom she liked, at that— she still found it impossible to remove herself voluntarily from the stimulation of his touch and continued to stand close by his side while only half listening to the conversation flowing around her.

'Will you have one too, Mark?' asked Lyla after pouring the squash into three plastic cups and, with brows enquiringly raised, prepared to gather another one from beneath the counter.

Mark moved his head negatively. 'No, thanks, Lyla. Each to his own,' he smiled, holding aloft in his free hand a can of beer already dappled with condensation and from which he proceeded to take a long and satisfactory draught.

Lyle accepted his refusal with wry grace. 'I should have known there were too many of you men congregating round the spits for you all to be interested in how the meat was faring.'

'Ah, but you surely wouldn't begrudge us a small reward for our efforts, would you?' he teased. 'It's hot work with those fires going.'

'As if any of you needed the excuse!' she retorted with a laugh.

Eve's entrance into the conversation put an end to the bantering exchange and had Shannon coming out of her daydream with all senses on the alert.

'Where's Hilary this morning, Mark?' she queried. 'I thought she would have been down here earlier than this. There's nothing wrong, is there?'

'No, nothing like that,' he returned easily. 'I'm sorry, I should have mentioned it before, but she rang me last night to say she had to drive into town this morning to meet somebody from the train. They'll be arriving later but, in the meantime, Austin brought all their contributions down when he came,' he explained.

'So that's it,' Eve nodded her understanding. 'I won-

dered, because when I was talking to her last Wednesday I
know she was planning to arrive early.' Her head tilted to
one side and she gave him an enquiring look. 'Who's she
meeting? Anyone we know?'

Mark took another drink from his can before answering.
'I don't think so—he comes from Sydney. A manager in the
pastoral company they deal with.'

The interest died from Eve's face. 'Oh, just a business
connection,' she exclaimed cursorily. 'I thought he might
have been an old classmate.'

'Sorry to disappoint you,' Mark grinned. 'Although you
might find . . .'

'Hey, Mark! Where did you put the microphone we're
supposed to use for the official announcements?' Pete's
shouted question cut short his brother's words and with a
rueful look Mark lifted one hand to the brim of his hat,
excused himself from his three companions and began striding between the groups of gaily dressed people thronging
the grounds to where Pete was waiting for him on the
school verandah.

Shannon sipped at her drink slowly, her eyes thoughtful
as they followed his departure. Was that the reason she had
been receiving his attention this morning? Because Hilary
wasn't there? Because he knew she wouldn't, or couldn't,
repel his advances and that she would—in a despairing
admission—willingly take the other girl's place if she
could? Was she just a convenient stopgap for him? Oh,
God! Her face clouded despondently. Fired or not, she
couldn't possibly stay at Tuesday any longer. She would
have to tell Mark she was leaving before he guessed the
truth and she suffered the greatest humiliation of her life.

Suddenly she felt a hand on her arm and could hear Eve
saying something about now being a good time for them to
have a thorough look at the exhibits.

'I beg your pardon?' she frowned in response at first,

then determinedly dragged herself out of her pensive reverie. 'Oh! Oh, yes, that's a good idea,' she conceded with a forced gaiety in order to dispel Eve's quizzical glance, and hastily continued with an apologetic evasion, "Sorry, I must have been off in a trance. Where do you suggest we start?' dropping her mug into the wire basket beside the stall.

'The tally books, I think,' recommended Eve, and over her shoulder, 'We'll see you later, Lyla. Keep up the good work,' she chuckled.

'As long as you don't forget to relieve me on time,' the other woman called after them goodnaturedly, which had Shannon and Eve trading laughing grimaces at the thought of their turns in serving drinks and refreshments yet to come.

Eventually, as Eve was required at another of the booths, it was Shannon who replaced Lyla at the drink stall after the official welcome had been extended by Mark in his capacity as President of the Committee, to all the former students and residents of the district, with photographs being taken of the oldest and youngest living pupils as they cut into an elaborately decorated cake together to commemorate the occasion, and when Guy—looking very much the part of the pioneer in his dark pants, woollen vest and battered hat—sauntered up to the counter she couldn't help laughing at the picture he made.

'What on earth are they?' she gurgled irrepressibly, pointing to the strings he had tied around each sturdy leg.

'Don't show your ignorance, my girl,' he retaliated in tones of mock disgust, a wide smile spreading over his face. 'They happen to be trusty bowyangs.'

'Bowyangs! But what are they for?' she demanded, still laughing.

His eyes rolled skywards sorrowfully. 'Shannon, Shannon! What are we going to do with you?' he tut-tutted in despair. 'They were to keep the vermin out, of course! Spiders ... snakes ... leeches,' he dwelt on each one devilishly.

'Ugh! Don't! What a horrible thought,' she shuddered, and changed the subject by fingering his woollen vest experimentally. 'I thought it was bad enough in this,' she indicated her long dress, 'but you must be roasting in that!'

Guy gave a rueful grin. 'They used to reckon they were good for soaking up the sweat, but after today I'm wondering if they didn't have things back to front somewhat—it was the vest causing the sweat in the first place!'

'But where did you get it from? I don't think I've ever seen one quite like that before.'

'Neither had I until my mother resurrected it from goodness knows where,' he owned with a grimace. 'I think it must have been her grandfather's.'

Shannon poured two drinks for a parched-looking blonde in heavy pink velveteen and turned back to him consolingly.

'Never mind, it's only for one day,' she said. 'At least we don't have to wear them all the time.'

His swift, 'Heaven forbid!' was ejaculated with such a spontaneous depth of feeling and with such a look of repugnance that Shannon burst into bubbling laughter once more at his expression, a sound which attracted many indulgent glances their way.

One look wasn't fond, though, as it swept over them and a decidedly grim Mark paced tigerishly towards the stall.

'Come on, Guy,' he urged aggressively. 'Isn't it about time you gave Tony a hand getting those camp ovens into the embers?' And after Guy had placidly given his acknowledgment, together with a knowing wink at Shannon, and gone ambling through the expanding crowd, he censured in sharp tones, 'Couldn't you conduct your love affair elsewhere? You're making people embarrassed at having to interrupt the pair of you.'

Shannon's lips pressed together hostilely at the unwarranted recrimination, but rather than attempt to deny it she chose instead to further it.

'Some,' her eyes pointedly travelled the length of him, 'don't seem to mind, though, do they?' she gibed, and turned her back on him in order to serve someone on the other side of the counter before he could reply.

By the time she swung back again Mark had disappeared and the anger that had been sustaining her quickly disintegrated, leaving only a hollow sense of hopelessness in its place. Obviously Mark was no closer to either forgiving, or forgetting, the circumstances under which she had arrived on his property, and it seemed every time he saw her with Guy it only served to remind him of the fact. She hunched her shoulders fretfully and was thankful when she was relieved of her duties and could escape from Mark's apparently watchful eyes and mingle indistinguishably among the crowd.

Not that someone with her looks could stay unnoticed for long, and it didn't present too great a problem for Betty Lovett to find her some ten minutes later so that she could whisper in a confidential way, 'Hilary's just arrived. Come and see what she's wearing.'

Shannon gave her excited companion a strange look. She supposed Hilary was wearing the yellow and green georgette she had said she would, but why that should inspire such animation within Betty's normally imperturbable self she couldn't imagine. It wasn't until they came closer to the smiling, laughing group of people surrounding Hilary that she began to suffer her first pangs of foreboding. There were too many people there for the gathering to have been occasioned by the wearing of a dress—no matter how eye-catching or beautiful it might have been. She could see Mark shaking hands with a smiling young man in his thirties whom she hadn't seen before—but who she deduced could have been the Donovans' visitor from Sydney—and there was Mrs Seymour, along with Hilary's father, as well as Pete and Beryl, and all appearing to be talking at the one time.

As Betty propelled her further into the throng she heard someone utter the word, 'Congratulations!' and her stomach plunged sickeningly to her feet. If that hadn't been enough, then Hilary's radiant face would have given the answer to the most dense of persons without her ever having to display the brilliant diamond cluster ring that sparkled on the third finger of her left hand.

Never would Shannon have believed she could act so convincingly as she did during the following minutes; offering her best wishes to Hilary as if she couldn't have been more pleased for the girl, and exclaiming with due enthusiasm over the beauty of her ring. But one thing she could not do, and that was to congratulate Mark. To retain her rigid self-control at the moment it was impossible to her to even contemplate taking the chance of looking at him, let alone speaking to him.

Her face a numbed mass of strained, smiling muscles, it was easy for her to edge her way backwards through the happy crowd—especially as more friends and acquaintances kept adding to the number—and begin walking, slowly at first but with increasing speed the further she left the gathering behind, towards the concealing trees that grew along the banks of the small creek which leisurely rippled its way across the bottom of the grounds behind the schoolhouse.

Here, uncaring that it might damage her dress, she slumped down on to a large fallen branch and, putting her head into her hands, she did something that all Mark's taunts and goadings hadn't been able to make her do—she cried, brokenly and defeatedly.

'For God's sake, Shannon! What on earth is going on between you and Guy that the mere sight of an engagement ring has you breaking down so uncontrollably?'

Mark's furiously spoken question was the first indication

Shannon had that she had been followed, and the shock of it was sufficient to momentarily halt the flow of tears and have her wiping her fingers anxiously over wet cheeks.

'What Guy and—and I do is our business ... not yours!' she attempted to discourage him, but most of the effect was lost by the quavering in her voice.

'The hell it's not!' She heard the sound of crunching twigs as he moved closer and stiffened apprehensively. 'Anything that happens on my property is my business,' he informed her arrogantly.

She sniffed and reminded him, 'We're not on your property,' in a rebellious mutter.

'Don't split straws with me, blue eyes!' she was warned inflexibly. 'Not at the moment! You're too vulnerable by half!'

It was the 'blue eyes' that did it. That once aggravating, but now suddenly endearing, term that was so uniquely Mark's that had the saltiness of tears stinging her eyes once more and she shook her head violently in rejection of its influence.

'Oh, why can't you just leave me alone, Mark?' she cried bitterly, chokingly, her arms wrapped comfortingly about her waist. 'Go back to your fiancée and leave *me* to settle my own affairs in my own way!'

For a moment she thought he had done what she had ordered so complete was the silence, but then an incredulous voice told her otherwise.

'What did you say?' he queried the ability of his own ears in disbelief.

'You heard me!' she stormed. 'I said, "go back to your fiancée and leave me to ..."'

'Hold it right there!' he commanded bluntly. 'Before we go any further, would you mind telling me just who my fiancée is?'

Shannon sucked in her breath sharply. 'I don't think that's very funny, Mark!' she reproved.

'Neither do I!' he agreed cynically. 'But if I'm to have a fiancée, I think it only fair that I should know her name, don't you?'

At last Shannon half turned to face him, a troubled frown creasing her forehead. 'But—but ... Hilary ...?' she stammered, uncertain now.

'Is marrying Bruce Kramer—the man she met at the station this morning.'

'Everyone said she would be marrying you.' She sounded accusing.

'Then they were wrong, weren't they?'

She shrugged with as much indifference as she could manage. 'Oh, well, I guess it doesn't matter much. It was nothing to do with me in any case,' she prevaricated, rising to her feet and moving further down the slope away from him.

'Shannon! Come back here!'

Her emotions too lacerated to sustain a cross-examination concerning her supposed affair with Guy, Shannon kept walking, ignoring the authoritative summons, but unable to refrain from shouting back, 'Go away, Mark! You have no right to try and run my life!' in what she hoped was a suitably imperious and squashing tone.

Maybe she should have known better than to try and outmatch him, but neither her thoughts nor her feelings were reacting normally at the moment, and when she heard his rapid footfalls gaining on her she spun to face him angrily, hands on hips, two glowing stains of colour high on her cheeks.

'Well? What now?' she demanded insolently. 'More sermons on my love life?'

'If the tears you were shedding back there are any indication, I'd say you needed some,' he commented sardonically as his steps slowed but didn't cease.

Even though she found herself forced to walk backwards so that she might keep some sort of distance between them, she continued to hold his glance defiantly and hurled at him disparagingly, 'But not from you! Or is this part and parcel of your responsibilities to your employees?' and without waiting for an answer, 'Well, I'm sorry, but I don't happen to want a father-confessor!'

'Have you any idea what you do want?'

Oh, yes, she had that all right, but with about as much chance as hell freezing over of achieving it. Her mouth tilted mockingly. 'Why? Are you planning to give me the benefit of your undoubtedly comprehensive experience and offer some suggestions?' she taunted.

There was no more than a foot or two separating them and it was an easy accomplishment for Mark's hand to grasp her inescapably by the nape of the neck.

'Suggestions?' he drawled, eyes sweeping indolently over her warily upturned face. 'No, I was thinking more on the lines of a demonstration. If nothing else, it might prove to you that your feelings for Guy aren't as strong as you seem to believe,' he advised lazily.

But it would also indicate just how strong they were in another direction and Shannon twisted her head against his curbing hand frantically in a desperate attempt to avoid the devastating touch of his lowering mouth.

'Don't you dare, Mark!' she ordered breathlessly, hands pushing against his chest ineffectively. 'It wouldn't prove a thing. I—I'm a natural two-timer ... you said so yourself, remember?' she grabbed at any excuse in her agitation.

'I also said you were a liar,' he reminded her softly in the split second before his lips found hers.

Her valiant efforts to resist the domination of his kiss melted traitorously beneath the increasing pressure and finally she stopped trying altogether. She was lost and she knew it! How could she hope to combat his attraction when she had so idiotically allowed him to become her very reason for living?

But the mounting passion which followed her surrender

brought its own tantalising rewards as she was held even closer to Mark's vital shape, the hard circle of his arms providing a protective security she had never before experienced, and his lips destroying her dissolving inhibitions with a consummate sensuousness. Suspended in time and thought, Shannon responded compliantly to his exploratory caresses, her breasts swelling beneath his warm hands, her mouth moving seductively against his, and her fingers hauntingly savouring the broad muscularity of his back.

Only when she regretfully felt his arms releasing her did complete consciousness return, but before she could find some plausible defence for her voluptuous capitulation, Mark had already broken the taut silence.

'What the hell are you trying to do to me, Shannon?' he exclaimed with a groan. 'Have you no idea of the thoughts that are running through my mind at this very moment?'

'That you wish I'd never come here? That you ought to let Guy know just what sort of a cheat I am?' she suggested bitterly.

'No! Damn you!' he dismissed her assumptions roughly, contemptuously almost. 'I was cursing Guy for having met you first, and myself for having fallen in love with you!' His hands bit into her shoulders convulsively. 'Make no mistake ... I want you, Shannon! I have ever since that first night when I saw you standing in the kitchen—looking as guilty as hell, but so utterly defenceless. You've played havoc with my emotions over these past months, blue eyes, but if I ever hold you in my arms like that again, there's no way I'll be able to vouch for my self-control!'

Shannon didn't know whether to laugh or cry with joy, and she made a choked sound that was a little of both as her hands slid shyly upwards over that wide chest and clasped lovingly about the back of his neck.

'Prove it,' she invited in a whisper.

Mark tensed, his hands coming up to cup her flushed face. 'And Guy?' he probed resolutely.

'It was you who kept insisting he meant something to me.'

'You said you cried yourself to sleep at night thinking about him,' he countercharged swiftly.

A mischievous smile lit her features. 'A slight exaggeration on my part,' she owned provocatively.

'I always said you were a deceiving little cat!' he groaned huskily, his eyes promising all kinds of delightful retribution as he effortlessly swung her into his arms and carried her to a patch of grass beneath a golden wattle where he lowered her gently to the ground. Leaning over, he stroked a thoughtful finger across soft lips. 'So why the tears over Hilary's engagement?'

'Can't you guess?' she replied ruefully. 'I thought *you* were her fiancé.'

His head moved from side to side slowly. 'Uh-uh! It's a scheming little impostor with the most beautiful eyes I've ever seen that I want to marry,' he told her with such a lazy curving smile that Shannon felt sure her heart would stop beating.

'Oh, Mark!' she sighed fervently, hands reaching up to draw his head closer. 'I love you so very much! I thought I would die when I saw that ring on Hilary's finger. I never knew I could feel so ferociously jealous of anyone in my life,' she admitted remorsefully.

With a wry look he declared gruffly, 'Then you'll understand how I felt seeing Guy kiss you when he arrived at the homestead, and for being able to make you laugh so happily when you were together at the drink stall.'

'Is that why you were so caustic?' She gave a delighted laugh at his confession, before assuring him with a grin, 'But I would have laughed at you too if you'd worn bowyangs! As for Guy kissing me—well, that was the first time ever and I certainly wasn't expecting it.' Her mouth pouted temptingly and her eyes twinkled with a teasing light. 'Would you like me to show you how I would really kiss the man I was in love with if I hadn't seen him for some months?' she enquired softly.

Mark's reply was conveyed in actions instead of words, and Shannon's hat soon found itself tossed carelessly on to the grass when lean fingers removed its securing pin and combed through her hair evocatively while firm lips demanded, and immediately received, an unhesitating response from her own.

Some tumultuous minutes later Mark relinquished his hold on her abruptly and moved away to grope shakily in his pocket for cigarettes and lighter, only remembering to offer Shannon one as an afterthought once he had lit his own.

'I'm sorry.' He shook his head disbelievingly at the oversight as she refused the outstretched packet. 'I'm afraid I'm not thinking any too straight at the present. I've got myself one formidable problem to solve.'

Shannon frowned as she sat up and curled her legs beneath her. 'What's that?' she asked, breath held nervously.

'How the hell am I going to survive until I can put a gold ring on your finger?' Which had her breath sighing between parted lips in relief and a flattering shade of pink suffusing her cheeks as she smiled up at him shyly. 'Up until now I've only found it *hard* to keep my hands off you,' he went on in the same dry tone, 'but I have the distinct impression that from here on I'm going to find it well nigh impossible!'

'Why didn't you say something before?'

'Because I thought you were too deeply involved with Guy.'

'Then why re-hire me?' she questioned interestedly. 'I certainly gave you enough reasons to send me packing.'

An arm across her shoulders pulled her close against his side and a reminiscent smile shaped his mouth. 'If you hadn't been so damned stubborn about accepting the

money for your fare back to the city I might have done ...
before I gave myself time for second thoughts. As it was, I
couldn't allow you to hitch-hike, so when Chris came to see
me that evening about keeping you on as our housekeeper—
well, I'm not sure which one of us was the more surprised
at the speed with which I accepted her suggestion.'

Loving eyes sparkled through long lashes. 'A decision I
think you regretted on more than one occasion,' she recalled
impishly.

'Who could blame me? Half the time I didn't know
whether I was on my head or my heels. First you denied
being anything but friends with Guy—then you were im-
plying a far closer association! But, in the meantime,
whenever I turned around there was Tony beside you, while
I...'

'Mmm, while you ...?' she urged mischievously.

'While I was denouncing myself for letting you get under
my skin in the first place! Too often it appeared you were
just as I'd described you—a double-dealing little liar, only
with an undermining ability to look innocently in need of
*pro*tection, rather than *cor*rection!'

'Is that what you wanted to do? Protect me?'

Mark's eyes roved over her expressively. 'Among other
things,' he drawled.

'Oh!' Shannon savoured the intensely thought-provoking
words in silence, then, in bantering retaliation, 'Except for
the instance when you wanted to wring my neck, of
course!'

'Except for then,' he allowed with an acknowledging
grin, his hand sliding down the curve of her throat tormentingly. It was all Shannon could do to keep her mind on
what she had been planning to say, but she pressed on
indomitably.

'You wouldn't let me have anything more to do with the
stock either!' she accused reproachfully. 'You might at

least have let me learn some of the fundamentals.'

'And thereby give you the experience to apply for a position elsewhere? Uh-uh!' He moved his head decisively. 'I preferred you ignorant ... but dependent!' He turned her face up to his and placed a lingering kiss on her lips. 'Not that I seem to have won that battle either. I happened to notice some very appealing sketches in Nola's studio last week of a young girl mounted on a roan horse,' he smiled down at her indulgently.

Of course! Nola had been round the yards with her sketchbook a few times of late. She should have realised it was possible she would have been used as a subject—everyone else had—and that Mark was likely to see them. She sighed and glanced at him contritely.

'I'm sorry, Mark,' she said earnestly. 'Please don't blame Tony—it wasn't his fault.'

'That I don't doubt,' he laughed. 'You forget, I know from personal experience just what effect those big blue eyes of yours can have on a man.'

Pleased that Tony wasn't about to be hauled over the coals for his part in her tuition, Shannon tilted her head to one side thoughtfully. 'Why *do* you always call me "blue eyes", Mark?' she questioned curiously.

Two warm hands cupped her face and a shapely mouth met hers for the second time in as many minutes. 'Because, my darling, they were the first insurmountable contributions to my downfall, and I love them as much as I do you.'

'You didn't always seem very charmed by them. In fact, one could almost assume you disliked them intensely at times,' she chuckled in remembrance.

'And you're surprised?' he returned incredulously. 'The drowsy invitation they contain when you've been kissed would be enough to defeat any man. My God! As your employer, I was supposed to be looking after your welfare, not subverting it!'

Shannon dimpled enchantingly. 'I did warn you that I couldn't consider you as a replacement father, didn't I?' she laughed.

'But you forgot to tell me you *could* consider me as a husband,' he murmured close beside the corner of her mouth. Shannon could only shake her head feebly.

'Those ideas I thought best to keep to my daydreams,' she whispered huskily. 'I didn't think I could ever have a chance of gaining your love. Especially not after the way I began on Tuesday, and—and believing you about to become engaged to Hilary.'

Mark smiled tenderly into her slightly misty eyes. 'You should have had more faith,' he remonstrated. 'Or did you think when I kissed you that I was cheating Hilary the same way I mistakenly believed you were cheating Guy?'

'Something like that,' she nodded with a woebegone expression at the memory.

'Well, I'll have you know, Shannon Marshall, that I don't two-time the girl I love!' He paused to issue the warning. 'But neither will I ever let her go! You see, I happen to believe in the increasingly passé "till death us do part" scene.'

Shannon twined her arms about him irresistibly. 'You'd better believe in it,' she threatened with a smile. 'Because that's the only thing that can part us now. I love you, Mark, and . . .'

The remainder was lost when Mark's lips sought hers yet again and all thought of explanations or declarations were forgotten in the ecstasy of the moment, but in the end it was Mark again who broke their embrace precipitately with a groan, rising to his feet in a single fluid action and raking a hand through his tousled hair.

'For the sake of your honour—and my self-restraint—I think it would be prudent if we left this secluded spot,' he suggested ruefully, bending to swing Shannon to her feet and restoring her hat to slightly trembling fingers.

Shannon nodded wordlessly, her breathing still shallow and erratic, and after a few fumbled attempts managed to return her boater to its original position before Mark's arm had caught her fast about the waist and together they began their return to the festivities with slow steps.

No sooner had they emerged from beside the schoolhouse than Nola hurried up to them, the worried look clearing from her face at their appearance. 'There you are!' she exclaimed. 'I've been looking everywhere for you. We're about to start the lunches.'

Whether it was something in their faces or merely the possessive arm holding Shannon close neither of them could guess, but Nola suddenly smiled and nodded her head complacently.

'It's about time there were more Seymours attending this school,' she propounded candidly before hurrying back in the same direction from which she had come.

Shannon and Mark glanced at each other and started to laugh. 'At times I don't think your mother is quite as imperceptive as she would have us believe,' smiled Shannon.

'You could be right,' Mark agreed lazily. 'But, more importantly, what did you think of her suggestion?'

'Well...' Shannon pretended to give the idea deep thought. 'As the Seymours have been here for the first hundred years, I suppose it is only fair that we should make an effort to see that they're around for the second hundred as well,' she proposed generously.

Mark's reaction came in the form of a tightening arm and a long finger tilting her head upwards. 'I'll keep you to that!' he advised deeply, his tawny eyes leaving her in no doubt as to the strength of his feelings, and Shannon knew that in the years to come it was a promise she would willingly fulfil.

In every issue...

Here's what you'll find:

❤ a complete, full-length romantic novel...illustrated in color.

❤ exotic travel feature...an adventurous visit to a romantic faraway corner of the world.

❤ delightful recipes from around the world...to bring delectable new ideas to your table.

❤ reader's page...your chance to exchange news and views with other Harlequin readers.

❤ other features on a wide variety of interesting subjects.

Start enjoying your own copies of Harlequin magazine immediately by completing the subscription reservation form.

Not sold in stores!